BLOWN AWAY!

Joan Hiatt Harlow

SCHOLASTIC INC.
New York Toronto London Auckland Sydney
Mexico City New Delhi Hong Kong Buenos Aires

No part of this publication may be reproduced, stored in a retrieval system, or transmitted in any form or by any means, electronic, mechanical, photocopying, recording, or otherwise, without written permission of the publisher. For information regarding permission, write to Margaret K. McElderry Books, an imprint of Simon & Schuster Children's Publishing Division, 1230 Avenue of the Americas, New York, NY 10020.

ISBN-13: 978-0-545-14037-9
ISBN-10: 0-545-14037-4

12 11 10 9 8 7 6 5 4 3 2 1   9 10 11 12 13 14/0

Printed in the U.S.A.   40

First Scholastic printing, January 2009

Book design by Sammy Yuen Jr.
Map by Niki Marion
The text for this book is set in Lomba Book.

Dedicated with love from Noanie to:
Anthony Edward Bilodeau, age three,
and
Richard Lee Clayter, age two

"Sweet little sleepyheads, close your eyes
To dream of a bright tomorrow,
With blue balloons and merry tunes
And never a tear or sorrow."

CONTENTS

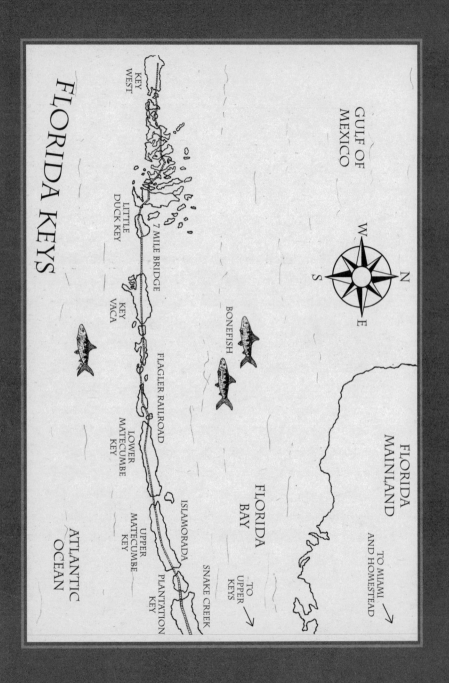

As I wandered along the shore of Islamorada that July morning in 1935, I didn't notice that I had reached the mangroves and sheltering sea-grape trees of the cove where old Sharkey lived. I was so intent on watching a manatee glide through the calm water that before I realized it, I was on the stretch of beach near Sharkey's place.

I was about to make a hasty exit when I saw a clearly defined row of turtle tracks in the sand and heard a familiar scratching noise. My gaze followed the tracks to the place where the sandy beach abutted the jungle-like foliage, and there I saw a huge raccoon eagerly digging, tossing the sand aside with his claws. He was after the turtle eggs.

"Scram! Get away from there!" I yelled, waving my arms and racing toward the raccoon. The animal hesitated, then turned and lumbered off into the brush. I bent down and smoothed the sand over the nest.

"Hey you, Jake Pitney! Leave that nest alone!" I looked up and there was Sharkey hobbling toward me and gesturing with his cane, a knotted stick of mahogany. His face was as red as a boiled crayfish.

Instinctively I put my arms up in front of me. "I wouldn't hurt the nest. I was just chasing a raccoon away from the eggs."

Sharkey glanced toward the nearby mangroves. "He'll be back. I've been trying to get rid of that robber for a long time. I tell you, between the coons and the cannery, there won't be a sea turtle left in a few years," he complained.

I stood there feeling guilty and not knowing what to say. At the lunch counter in our family's general store we served turtle soup from the cannery.

"I've got a panther prowling around here too. See those tracks?" He pointed to another set of prints in the damp earth beneath the trees.

I had to look closely to make them out in the mud. "Could those be a dog's?" I asked.

"There's no dog around here *that* size,"

Sharkey snorted. "Besides, if they were dog tracks, there'd be claws showing in the tracks. Cats have retractable claws. I've heard the panther cater-wauling at night. He'll probably go after the eggs too. This is the second nest that turtle's laid since the coon ransacked the last one."

Sharkey looked around and pointed with his cane at a broken-down rowboat. "Give me a hand with that old tub. I sure can't stand around here day and night guarding that nest."

I wanted to get out of there, so I quickly grabbed the bow end while he took the stern and we turned the boat upside down over the turtle nest. "That should protect it for now. But when the hatchlings head for the water, the gulls will proba-bly swoop down and grab 'em anyway. It's a losing battle." He sat on the boat and glowered at me from under his bushy eyebrows.

That was my signal to leave. I knew firsthand how Sharkey yelled and chased kids off his prop-erty with his cane, and I wasn't going to stick around to see it again. I began to back away toward the path to town.

"Hey, wait just one darn minute!" Sharkey

ordered. I stopped dead still as he opened up a pocketknife. "What do you do in your spare time?"

"I—I fish a lot," I stammered.

Sharkey reached into his shirt pocket, pulled out a small piece of wood, and began whittling. "I need someone to help me out with work," he went on, "like caulking my boats and throwing some paint on my house." He gestured behind us with his thumb.

I glanced back and could see the roof of his place through the brush. Sharkey's home was an old boxcar that had been abandoned years ago, while Sharkey was working on the overseas railroad from Miami to Key West. The story goes that when the railroad was finished, the boxcar was forgotten, tucked away in the brush. So Sharkey just helped himself to it and moved on in. Folks said Sharkey had some money from his veteran's pension and could probably afford a bungalow somewhere, but he seemed content in his freight car.

The boxcar wasn't much to look at, but it sheltered Sharkey from the crosswinds that blew from the Atlantic on one side and Florida Bay on the other. Where it was rusted, Sharkey had slapped on a few coats of leftover paint he got from our general store. It was smeared with bright yellow and red and a few streaks of blue here and there. We must have had a sale on one color, because most of the car was now a sickening pickle green. One good thing about that shade was that it blended in under the big round leaves of the sea-grape trees.

It was strange. Although we kids were scared of Sharkey, the grown-ups around town all liked and respected him. Even my dad. I remember how he stood up for Sharkey when our neighbor, Mr. Ashburn, complained about his ugly old freight car. Dad had reasoned, "Hey, Sharkey worked hard for years putting that railroad through. If it weren't for guys like him, that overseas railway from Miami to Key West would have never been built. Since no one from the railroad ever claimed that boxcar, why shouldn't Sharkey put it to some use?"

Sharkey blew the dust from the piece of wood he was whittling. "I was hunting gators in the glades last week, but I came back early to nurse my leg along."

I'd always wondered what was wrong with Sharkey's leg. He had been a wrecker, so I thought he might have been hurt diving down into sunken ships to retrieve merchandise. Dad said he was wounded in the Great War, while some of the other kids said Sharkey had been a pirate and was injured in a fight. We pictured him in his earlier days with a patch over one eye, brandishing a sword. More reason to believe he was a pirate was that gold-coin necklace he always wore. Tough guys like Sharkey didn't wear necklaces, so we were pretty sure it was part of his pirate stash. When I mentioned it to Mom, she said it was probably a religious medal, but Sharkey didn't seem like the religious type. We couldn't get a good look at it, but we'd seen it glitter on his hairy chest, and it looked like real gold.

Sharkey shifted his leg, and I could see he was in pain. "Dang leg! I need to be able to fish by fall when the rich guys come back," he said. "Those millionaires tip well when they have a good fishing catch."

Sharkey worked as a guide for the Millionaires Club, a resort on the ocean side of our town,

Islamorada. He was a popular guide because he knew where the bonefish or tarpon would be running.

I was still wondering if Sharkey wanted me to work for him, when he finally came right out and said, "Anyway, I could use a hand with my gator hides." He wiped the small sculpture in his hand with a handkerchief, and I could now see that it was a first-rate likeness of an alligator. "I need someone to go to Key West on the train with me tomorrow."

"Are you offering me a job?"

"Of course I am. What do you think I'm talking about here?"

"You said you needed *someone*. You didn't say *who*," I retorted.

Sharkey shook his head. "Well, I meant you."

I wondered if he would pay me. Then, as if reading my mind, Sharkey said, "I'll pay you as soon as I sell the hides. It won't be a lot, but I would think a kid like you could use some spare change. So, what's your answer?" he demanded. "Are you taking the job or not?"

Did I really want to go to Key West with

someone as cantankerous as Sharkey? "I need to ask my folks."

"I'll go over to the store later today and talk to your dad."

"Okay," I said, still in shock. A trip to Key West with Sharkey might be a real adventure. Why not?

I raced back along the overgrown path and onto the dirt road, leaving Sharkey standing by the beach watching me.

Wait until the other Islamorada kids hear this, I thought as I made a beeline toward town. They'll never believe that I'm going to Key West with old Sharkey himself!

I raced onto the porch steps of our store and burst through the screen door, letting it slam behind me. We had a lunch counter and a few tables in our general store, and Mom was serving coffee and sandwiches to a couple of the veterans who'd come to work on the new highway from Miami to Key West.

"Jake! Where have you been?" she called out to me. "I'm real busy, and I need you to watch Star." She nodded toward a table where my three-year-old sister was finishing up her lunch. "She's been fussy this morning and needs to take a nap. Take her upstairs." Mom handed me a bologna sandwich and a glass of milk. "Here's your lunch. Eat it up in the kitchen. And don't spill anything on—"

"On the rug. I know, I know." Mom's most valued possession was the "genuine American Oriental rug" that covered our living room floor. She'd had it shipped here all the way from her home back in Georgia when she moved to the Keys. "Mom, can I go to Key West tomorrow with Sharkey?"

Mom looked at me in surprise. "With Sharkey? Did he ask you?"

"Yes. He needs me to help him carry his gator hides."

"No. I need you here."

"Please, Mom. He's going to pay me, and I can use the money."

Mom shook her head. "Not tomorrow." She wiped Star's face with a cloth and pointed her toward the stairway.

"Come on, Mom," I begged.

"Aw, let him go, Louella," said Milt Barclay, one of the Bonus Marchers, as the veterans working on the highway were known.

"Yeah, a kid his age needs to get around more," his buddy, Harry Webber, agreed. He turned to me. "How old are you. Fifteen or so?"

"I'll be fourteen in December," I told him.

"If you don't let a boy loose once in a while, he'll break free on his own one of these days," Milt said.

"And then you'll have a real problem on your hands, Louella," Harry added.

Mom's mouth tightened. If looks could kill, both those men would have fallen over dead right there and then. Scowling, she wiped off the counter with a vengeance. Then she sighed. "I guess it's okay with me. But you'll need to ask your father."

I gave the two men a grateful smile as I headed toward the stairs with Star. Now I only had Dad to deal with.

Once upstairs I took off my shoes so I wouldn't track dirt onto Mom's precious rug. While I ate my sandwich in the kitchen, Star brought her book, *Wind and Stars and Bright Blue Skies*, for me to read to her. She climbed into my lap and opened the book.

"I'm only reading one poem," I told her. I flipped the pages looking for the shortest one. "This is nice." I pointed to the illustration of a child in bed with fairies dancing around. I hoped Star would get the point and go to sleep. "'The soft breeze through the window makes the gauzy curtains dance,'" I read quickly, "'while all across the ceiling the nighttime fairies prance.'"

"That's a nighttime poem," Star whined. "It's not nighttime!"

"Okay, okay," I said, reading the verse again rapidly. "'The soft breeze through the window makes the gauzy curtains dance, while all across the ceiling the *naptime* fairies prance.'" I slammed the book shut. "Now go to bed."

"You didn't read it right, and you only read one verse." Star began to cry loudly.

"Jake!" Mom yelled from downstairs. "Be good to her!"

"Go to your bedroom, Star," I said. "I'll read you another poem in there."

She slipped off my lap and toddled into her bedroom. I followed her, and she climbed into the bed. Then I opened the windows and closed the blinds. The soft, salty breeze swept in from the ocean and puffed her white curtains like a cloud.

"See?" Star whispered with a yawn. "The wind is making my curtains dance too."

"Pick out another poem," I said, passing her the book.

"This one," she said. "I love this one." She pointed to the picture of a boy sending a toy boat off onto the water, then handed the book back to me. "Don't read fast."

> I sent my boat upon the waves;
> The breeze filled up her sail.
> Then far away it took my ship
> Into the wildest gale.
> My little craft moved bravely out
> Over the stormy sea.
> I wonder if my ship will find
> Its way back home to me.

Star's eyes began to close. Her hair was damp with sweat and stuck in little curls around her face. She burrowed into her pillow and closed her eyes.

I tiptoed quietly out of her room, grabbed my shoes, then flew downstairs two steps at a time. "Star's asleep," I told Mom, who was clearing the table where the veterans had eaten their lunch. They were gone now, and the store was empty. "Where's Dad?" I asked, putting on my shoes.

"He's meeting the one o'clock train. We're expecting a shipment of supplies from Homestead."

A small white building up the road had served as the Islamorada post office until the overseas railroad from Miami to Key West began chugging through back in 1912. Since then, it had served as both the post office and the train station. Now folks could send and trade supplies back and forth from Islamorada down to Key West or up to Miami by boxcar instead of by boat. Soon the vets would have our new highway built too, and we'd be able to go up and down the string of islands by car.

Dad was standing by the tracks, his hands on his hips, as the train pulled into the station. I ran to join him just as a railroad man began piling boxes by the side of the tracks. Dad and I stacked them in the back of the truck. "Good," Dad commented as he checked the stenciled information on the cartons. "We needed this merchandise. And the Ashburns have been waiting for their new fishing gear."

"Dad . . . ," I said breathlessly. "Can I go to Key West with Sharkey tomorrow? Mom said to ask you."

"I just bumped into Sharkey on my way here, so I've already talked with him. I said it would be all right if your mom gave permission."

"I can go, then!"

"You're going to help Sharkey, so don't get the idea it's a joyride."

"I won't. I'll help Sharkey cart the gator hides and do whatever else he needs."

"I'll tell Sharkey you can go," Dad said. He got into the cab, started the engine. "Want a ride back?"

"No, I'm going to see Roy and Billy." I headed down to the ocean side, where the Ashburn family lived. Their house was on the south side of the famous Millionaires Club, which was maintained by Leon Ashburn, Billy and Roy's father. As care-taker, Mr. Ashburn was able to hitch up to the club's electricity, and this gave them refrigeration, electric fans, and other luxuries year-round. They even had real toilets inside the house, not out-houses like most of the bungalows on the island. The Ashburns also had a nice tomato crop, a grove of lime trees, and a tract of pineapples. They packaged the fruits and sent them by train to the farmers' market up in Homestead, fifty miles or so north of us.

Both boys were fishing off their pier when I arrived. Their little sister, Bessie, was digging in the sand and filling the hole with water from a bucket. Bessie was about the same age as Star, and they often played together. "Hi, Jake," Bessie said, looking up. "Where's Star?"

"She's home," I answered. Bessie went back to her digging.

Their dog, Ginger, who was sitting next to Bessie, barked and came to meet me. "Hey, Jake!" Roy called. "We got something to tell you."

"We're gonna have a fishing contest!" Billy yelled. "All the kids in Islamorada can enter the contest, and whoever gets the best fish wins."

I ran down the pier to the boys with Ginger at my heels. "What kind of fish?" I asked breathlessly.

"Any kind—except mudfish don't count," Roy said, casting his line and fly into the waves.

"And if someone bags a bonefish, they'll automatically win," Billy added.

Bonefish are the fastest and smartest fish ever—real fighters and hard to catch. I knew of a place they fed in schools, on the flats over on the bay side. "What's the prize?"

"Our dad said he'll take the winner to Miami next week on the train," said Roy.

"And to a movie show," Billy added.

I sure would love to win, I thought. I hardly ever got to see a movie. "When's the contest?"

"As soon as the gear we ordered comes in," Billy said.

"Dad said your fishing equipment came in today," I told them.

"Let's go up to the store and get our new poles," Roy said, reeling in his line.

Billy pulled in his fishing rod too. "We can have the tournament Friday—tomorrow."

"Not tomorrow!" I protested. "I'm going to Key West with Sharkey tomorrow."

Both kids looked like they'd been shocked by an eel. Their mouths dropped open and their eyes bugged out. "With *Sharkey*?" they gasped in unison.

"Yep," I said. "I'm working for him now."

"Since when?" Roy looked unconvinced.

"Since today. He and I talked about it this morning."

Again the boys' eyes widened. "That won't be any fun," Billy said.

"He's too mean and grumpy," Roy added. "He yells at us and chases us away every time we as much as pass by his stupid-looking hut."

"He never did that until he caught you snooping around his place last year," I reminded him. I had heard the story a dozen times or more.

"And Roy tried to hide in his rain barrel," Billy said with a laugh. "There you were, Roy, up to your nose in water. It's a wonder you didn't drown. I'll never forget how you squirmed and kicked and splashed when Sharkey pulled you out."

"You were a big help, hiding in the bushes," Roy complained. "And then Sharkey made me clean out his old rain barrel."

"That rain barrel was the only fresh water he had, and you ruined it jumping in with your dirty shoes on," I said. "I'm glad I wasn't there."

"Just listen to Jake stick up for his new buddy Sharkey," Roy said to his brother. "And now he's going off to Key West with him tomorrow."

"So you can't be in our tournament, then," Billy said.

I started to walk away. "That's too bad, 'cause I know I'd win."

"What makes you so sure?" Roy asked scornfully.

"I'd catch a nice fat bonefish, and—as you said—a bonefish wins." I headed up the wharf toward shore, walking slowly. I was hoping they'd take my challenge and hold off on their contest. I wanted to be in the competition really badly, but by now Dad had probably told Sharkey I could go with him on Friday, and I sure didn't want to make Sharkey mad.

I looked back and could see Roy and Billy with their heads together. Then Roy yelled out, "Okay, Jake. The contest will start on Saturday morning and end at noon. That will give us all day tomorrow to practice with our brand-new gear, and then you'll see who wins!"

Mom packed sandwiches, a thermos of orange juice, and some paper cups in a sack. "In case you or Sharkey gets hungry on the way," she said.

Sharkey told Dad that he'd meet me at the train station Friday morning, where we'd catch the eight o'clock train to Key West. I was excited but uneasy. Sharkey was the grumpiest and most unfriendly person I'd ever met.

At the station Sharkey was leaning on his cane and waiting with a knapsack and a huge wheelbarrow full of dried alligator hides. He wore a short-sleeved plaid shirt, tan pants, and a straw hat that tied under his chin. "'Bout time!" he hollered when he saw me. "We need to get these hides on board. And we'll take the wheelbarrow, too. It'll be handy for stuff I might buy."

When the train chugged into the station, we heaved the hides and the barrow into the freight car, and then we took seats in the smoking car. By the time we boarded, the car was almost full with loud veterans from the highway project. Friday meant payday, and this group was on its way to Key West for a good time, as my dad would say.

I held the lunch in my lap. "Want a drink?" I asked Sharkey over the din.

"Not right now." The seat in front of us was empty, so Sharkey reversed it, shoved his knapsack under it, then put his bad leg up on the seat. "Might as well get comfortable. It's a long ride from Islamorada. About eighty miles, I'd say."

"If we go sixty miles an hour, we should be there in an hour and a half or so," I said. "That's not too long."

As soon as the train started, it seemed as if everyone in the car lit up a cigarette. The man across the aisle from us was chomping on a cigar.

"I'm going to the other car," I told Sharkey. "The smoke is making me sick."

"Sit down. Don't be a sissy."

"You don't want me to throw up, do you?" I said sharply.

Sharkey shrugged. "Oh, go ahead," he answered crustily. He lay back and pulled his hat over his face. "Wake me when we get there."

I took the bag of sandwiches and stepped out onto the platform between cars. I stayed outside breathing in the salty air. The Flagler railway from Miami to Key West was called the eighth wonder of the world. No one had thought an ocean railway could ever be built, but Mr. Flagler made it happen.

I was beginning to feel better and was enjoying the ride, when the door to the car opened and Sharkey came out in a cloud of blue smoke, carrying his knapsack.

"I thought you were sleeping," I said.

He stood next to me, squinting out at the view. "Couldn't sleep. My leg's bothering me."

"How did you hurt it, anyway? Dad said it happened in the war."

"That's right. After the railroad was finished and the Great War began, I joined the army. Some German Jerry got in a good shot over in France. The bullet went into the bone. I was in the hospital for months and couldn't wait to get back to the Keys. My old boxcar never looked so good as the day I came home. But the leg's bothered me ever since."

We stayed on the platform between cars, listening to the clicking of the wheels and watching the dark-blue Atlantic on the left and the turquoise Florida Bay on the right as we moved from one Key to another. My town of Islamorada is on Upper Matecumbe Key, about halfway down to Key West. Now we were dashing over the lower Keys—all of them like jewels on the sea.

When we crossed the Seven Mile Bridge, I held my breath. I'd crossed the bridge several times, but each time it was as if the sky and sea melded together and the whole world was shining and blue. I was sure that nowhere on earth was there such a miracle as the seven-mile-long bridge that Mr. Flagler had built right out on the sea, and which seemed to be disconnected to the rest of the earth.

After a while we went into the forward car and ate our lunch. Sharkey took a bite of the thick sandwich and spilled some on his shirt. "Egg salad," he muttered. "Too messy."

Sharkey had some nerve to complain about Mom's sandwiches! "Better than nothing," I answered brusquely.

"Yep, a whole lot better than nothing," Sharkey agreed.

Key West was a busy, bustling port filled with ships flying the American flag at the top of their masts and the flags of other nations beneath it. Catches from fishing vessels were being unloaded, and the smell of fish filled the air. In another area of the port, fancy white yachts were hitched to the docks while their well-dressed passengers and crew meandered through the town.

Sharkey and I pushed the wheelbarrow full of hides to a place where people were trading and exchanging goods. "Hey, Sharkey!" folks yelled as we passed by, and Sharkey nodded or gave a small salute. I was surprised to see how well known he was here in Key West.

We stopped at a booth where Sharkey emptied a bag of wooden figurines he had in his backpack onto the table. "Carved 'em myself," I heard him say. "Good for souvenirs."

They were amazingly good! Some were of gators, some of fish, and there was a real pretty one of a leaping dolphin. The man at that booth handed Sharkey a wad of bills and took the entire batch. I was impressed that Sharkey, a hunter and fisherman, was also a talented artist. He sure was popular around here. And folks around Key West seemed to respect him.

The kids back home looked at Sharkey in a very different way—a fearful, run-when-you-see-him kind of way. Of course, he did catch the Ashburn boys spying on him, so I guess you couldn't blame Sharkey for being crabby. The Islamorada kids often spied on him or sneaked around his property.

At a large tent a man came out and talked with Sharkey. Then he looked over the pile of hides, carefully examining each one. While the two men argued about prices and quality, I meandered around the area checking out souvenirs, fishing gear, and leather wallets and belts.

Soon Sharkey caught up with me. He set the empty wheelbarrow down and stuffed another wad of bills in his pocket. "I'm all set." He seemed satisfied. "Let's take a look at the auctions."

Sharkey explained that the auctions were sales of overstocked or damaged goods that wreckers had salvaged from shipwrecks and brought to Key West to sell.

We passed by places where folks had gathered in small groups to bid on everything from bolts of cloth to kapok life jackets that had been pulled from sunk or sinking ships. Then I noticed a crowd of people looking over a mule that was tied to a nearby post.

"You'll be surprised to see how much pack this here little mule can carry," a man crowed. He appeared to be the owner. "She can pull a wagon as well as any horse. She's strong and good-mannered."

"She's a mule, Frank!" someone snorted. "They don't have good manners."

"They're not sissified fancy horses," Frank snapped back. "They're workers, and they don't have time to prance around."

The pretty brown and white spotted mule stood quietly, her tail switching at flies. As

Sharkey limped over to get a better look, I swear she blinked her eyelashes at him. "Will she take a saddle?" Sharkey asked as he ran his fingers through the animal's thick coat.

"Why, sure she will. I'll even throw her saddle in with the sale." The man eyed Sharkey's limp. "Someone like you could use a good working animal like this. You can ride her or hitch her up to a cart and she'll pull you around nice as pie."

The mule moved closer to Sharkey and leaned against him. I was getting nervous. I'd heard how mules could kick in any direction at a moment's notice. This mule seemed calm enough, though. In fact now she was leaning her head on Sharkey's shoulder and nuzzling his neck.

"How old is she?" Sharkey asked, rubbing the soft spot between her ears.

"Fifteen or so. Used to work for the railroad."

"She's older than fifteen if she worked for the railroad," Sharkey scoffed. "Will she lift her legs for shoeing?"

"'Course!" Frank must have thought Sharkey was a good prospect, as he stopped speaking to the rest of the crowd and gave Sharkey his full attention. "Her name's Jewel," he said. "I love her like a child—I swear she's a sweetheart—but I can't keep her anymore."

"Why not?" Sharkey asked.

"Costs too much to feed her—" Frank stopped short when he realized his mistake. "Actually, she doesn't eat a lot." He backtracked. "A bag or two of oats every day. She works hard, and she's worth her keep."

"But you can't afford her," Sharkey retorted with a hard look at the man.

"Ah—well, er—" Frank stammered. "I'm retiring. Don't need a mule anymore."

"How much do you want for her?"

The owner's eyes widened. "She's a bargain at five hundred dollars."

Sharkey hobbled away without another word. I headed after him.

"You can have her for three hundred fifty," Frank called out.

"Let's go," Sharkey said to me, limping at his top speed.

"You don't really want the mule, do you?" I

asked breathlessly, hurrying to catch up while steering the clumsy wheelbarrow.

"Naw, I don't want her," he answered over his shoulder.

"Three hundred!" Frank yelled.

We kept walking.

Suddenly Frank cried out in a loud, sad voice. "Since no one wants to buy Jewel, I'll have to get rid of her. My poor, sweet mule will have to be put down."

Sharkey stopped dead in his tracks, and I stumbled into him, nearly knocking him over with the wheelbarrow. He pushed me aside and swung around. "One hundred dollars!" he bellowed, waving his cane.

"Sold!" Frank sang out. "You just bought yourself a mule!"

I was flabbergasted. Hadn't Sharkey said he didn't want the mule? But there he was handing out a hundred dollars for Jewel. He motioned for me to come, and he dumped the saddle into the wheelbarrow.

"You push the barrow," he told me, "and I'll lead the mule down to the train station. Will she ride in the baggage car okay?" he asked Frank, who was counting the money again.

"Sure. But you might stay with her back there. She could get lonely."

Sharkey took hold of the lead that was attached to Jewel's bridle and gave it a tug. "Come on, girl," he said. "We're going home."

Jewel just stood there, looking at us with those dark, sleepy eyes, and wouldn't budge.

"Come on, Jewel," Sharkey said in a command-ing voice. "Get going!"

Now this was worth watching. Sharkey had the reputation of being one tough hombre, as they said in the cowboy movies. No one could put any-thing over on him—least of all a mule. He gave her a tap on her flank. "Giddap!" he yelled. But Jewel simply ignored him. Several men nearby snick-ered, and Sharkey's face began turning red.

"What's wrong with this animal?" he yelled.

Frank looked up at Sharkey. "Not a thing," he said matter-of-factly. "She just doesn't go any-where without Rudy."

"Who in the name of all that's holy is Rudy?" Sharkey demanded.

The man looked around. A rust-colored dog was sleeping under a nearby table. "There he is. Hey, Rudy, come here, boy." The dog lifted his head drowsily and wagged a long silky tail. "I named him after the radio singer. You know, Rudy Vallee." Slowly Rudy pulled himself up, sauntered over to us, and sat. "Rudy, shake hands with this nice gentleman here."

The dog obediently lifted its paw, but Sharkey didn't respond. Instead he glared at Frank and shouted, "What has this dog got to do with the mule?"

The man grinned sheepishly. "Rudy is Jewel's buddy. They're a pair. Jewel loves that dog."

"You're telling me that if I take the mule . . ." Sharkey began.

"You have to take the dog. One's no good without the other."

Sharkey's face went from red to purple, and I was certain Frank was about to get a punch in the nose. But the dog, who was still sitting at Sharkey's feet, held his paw up again, tapping Sharkey on the leg and tilting his head quizzically.

I set the wheelbarrow down and petted Rudy. "He has a nice face. And he'd be good at scaring off the coons and that panther back home," I said cheerfully.

"Well, I was gonna sell him for a few bucks . . ." the man began.

"I'm not paying one extra cent for that dog," Sharkey declared with a warning glare.

". . . but you can have him at no extra charge,"

Frank quickly added. He hitched a leash to Rudy's collar and handed it to Sharkey. "Remember, pal, good things always come in pairs!"

So we ended up trudging down the narrow streets of Key West with Sharkey leading Jewel, me pushing the wheelbarrow, and Rudy running along ahead of us, stopping now and then to sniff at a tree or a fence.

When we got to the train, we looked at each other. How would we get Jewel into the boxcar? A trainman sized up the situation and found a ramp. But Jewel wouldn't get near the thing. I pulled on her bridle and Sharkey pushed from the rear. Still she wouldn't move.

"Get Rudy on the ramp," I suggested. "Come here, boy," I called. Rudy looked at me and then sat down next to Jewel.

Sharkey scratched his head, then his beard. "What a numbskull I am," he mumbled. "Spending good money on a couple of duds."

By now several passengers about to get on board were watching our attempts to get the animals into the boxcar.

"Light a fire under the mule," one man joked.

"It wants to sit in the passenger car!" another fellow scoffed.

Then I noticed a nearby refreshment stand with a sign that read HOT DOGS FIVE CENTS.

"Wait here," I said to Sharkey, and I pulled a nickel from my pocket and ran to the food cart. I handed my nickel over to a man in a striped apron and placed my order. "One hot dog. Plain."

"Here, Rudy," I called, frankfurter in hand. I held a piece out for him to sniff. Rudy stood up, tail wagging, and took it gently from my hand. "Come on, boy." Breaking off more pieces of hot dog, I lured Rudy up the ramp and into the freight car. He followed me happily, munching away.

Once Rudy was in the car, Jewel took a step onto the ramp, cautiously, as if she were testing its strength. I held my breath and glanced at Sharkey, who watched with his mouth open. We both waited silently, and then slowly, slowly, Jewel made her way up the ramp to the open freight car.

Sharkey climbed in after her, and on the return trip to Islamorada we stayed with Jewel and Rudy in the car with the baggage and freight. After several miles Rudy curled up and went to sleep, and within a few minutes Jewel folded her legs and lay down next to him. In the dim light I could see a flicker of a grin pass over Sharkey's face.

"Perhaps you should have put the saddle on Jewel and ridden her before you bought her," I said. "She looks smaller than a horse. You might not fit on her." I envisioned Sharkey on the mule with his feet dragging on the ground.

"She's almost fifteen hands," he snapped, "the size of a horse. Besides, I'll use her for pulling in boats and moving heavy stuff more than riding. Listen here, I took care of mules when I was in the army, long before you were born, and I know how to handle them. In fact Jewel reminds me of my favorite one. Her name was Sally." He scowled at me, and then he reached over and patted Rudy's head. Rudy responded by creeping close to Sharkey and leaning his head on Sharkey's good leg.

Now I understood why Sharkey had bought Jewel. She reminded him of Sally. It was kind of weird to think of Sharkey being fond of anything. He didn't speak again for a long while. Finally I said, "I'm entering the fishing contest tomorrow."

"I didn't hear of any contest," Sharkey said. "Who set it up?"

"The island kids. It's just for kids."

"What kind of fish?"

"Anything except mudfish. A bonefish beats everything."

"Even tarpon?"

"Aw, it's just a silly one-day contest. We don't expect to get tarpon or sailfish. But I'd sure like to bag a bonefish. I know a place where they feed over—" I stopped. No sense in telling everything I know. Sharkey might take the millionaires over there and fish the place out.

Sharkey's mouth twitched. He knew I wasn't about to give away the location of my secret place. "What's the prize for winning the contest?"

"A trip to Miami and a movie."

"You just had a trip to Key West," Sharkey said with a snort. Rudy lifted his head, startled, then snuggled on his good leg again. "Of course, we didn't see a movie." He stroked Rudy's ears.

I laughed. "Watching you bid for the mule was better than a movie."

"Humph! Very funny." He was silent for a

moment, then to my surprise added, "Come over after supper and I'll loan you a fly—a good one for bonefish."

So Sharkey really did use a fly for bonefish— probably his own invention. I heard he made some fancy flies. But I also heard that Sharkey was so fast he could spear one of those lightning-fast bonefish without a rod at all.

Sharkey scratched his beard. "If you're going for bonefish, you really should have a guide."

I knew only too well that it helped consider- ably to have a guide stand in the boat and spot the silver flashes of bonefish as they skittered through the water. "I don't have a guide," I told him.

"Tell you what," Sharkey continued, "if you come over tomorrow morning and give me a hand with Jewel, I'll teach you how to bag a bonefish." He leaned back against a stack of fishing tarps. "Of course, I'm not spending the whole day with you," he added, back in his grumpy voice. "Just an hour or so. Then you'll be on your own."

"Um. Sure, thanks," I agreed. Even though Sharkey could be the grouchiest man on earth at times, I was beginning to warm up to him. Why, he was going to teach me how to fly-fish, for Pete's sake! Yep, having Sharkey help me hook a bone-fish sounded like a real good deal to me.

The train stopped at Islamorada right on time, and Dad was there with the truck to meet us. I'll never forget the look on his face when we paraded Jewel and Rudy down the ramp and onto the dirt road.

"Am I seeing right?" Dad asked.

"You're seeing right, Dad!" I yelled, pushing the tipsy wheelbarrow, with the dog trotting along behind me. "Sharkey bought a mule and a dog in Key West!" Sharkey led Jewel nicely this time. The mule was probably tired of the train ride and eager to keep Rudy in her sights.

"She's a pretty thing, isn't she?" Sharkey said proudly as Jewel nuzzled his arm.

"Her name's Jewel," I told Dad. "The dog came with her. His name's Rudy."

"My game leg's been bothering me, and I

thought the mule could help pull the boats in when they need work—that kind of thing," Sharkey explained.

"I suppose a mule could come in handy," Dad agreed.

"Mules have put this whole country together," Sharkey went on, somewhat defensively, as if he had to explain that he wasn't totally crazy to have come home with Jewel. "They took the pioneers out West, they built the Erie Canal . . ."

"They work in the coal mines," an unfamiliar girl's voice piped up. "I've seen them down there hauling the coal cars. Some of them have never seen the light of day." The girl was sitting on the steps of the train station. Beside her was a battered cardboard suitcase that looked as though it might fall apart at any moment. I wondered if she was traveling by herself.

She went up to Jewel and petted her nose. Jewel seemed to like it. "Excuse me. I couldn't help overhearing. I love mules, as you can probably tell. And this one is pretty, and sweet, too." The girl's long red hair, which was held back with a white headband, reminded me of Rudy's tail. I felt a bit ashamed when the thought crossed my mind; comparing a girl's hair to a dog's tail wasn't very nice. But Rudy's tail was beautiful—long and silky—and the girl's hair, which fell to her waist, was long and silky too.

"I was to meet my aunt Edith here, but she's late. Can you tell me how to find Edith Kraynanski's house?" she asked.

Dad and I looked at each other in surprise. Edith Kraynanski was a Polish lady who had lived alone in her tidy little house for as long as I could remember. She was known for the delicious Polish food that she often shared with her neighbors. We never knew she had any family. "I'll show you where she lives," I offered. "But first I should help Sharkey with the mule and the dog."

"I'll give Sharkey a hand," Dad offered. "After you take . . ." He paused.

"Mara," the girl said, holding out her hand. "Mara Lynn Kraynanski."

"How do you do, Mara," Dad said, shaking her hand. "I'm Doug Pitney, and this is my son, Jake. We live at the general store down the road apiece, and your aunt Edith lives near us." He turned to me. "Jake, take Mara's suitcase and show her to Miss Edith's place. I'll help with the mule until you can get back to Sharkey's."

"Yeah, it'll take some doing to get these animals situated," Sharkey agreed.

"Thank you." Mara smiled at me gratefully.

I took her suitcase. "Come on. Miss Edith's place is just up the road a way. One thing about Upper Matecumbe Key is that it's a narrow island, so everything is pretty close together in the town of Islamorada. Folks live on one side of the tracks or the other. These railroad tracks were built up so high above the main road, we think of them as hills."

Mara laughed. "You should see the hills in Pennsylvania, where I come from!"

We walked along quietly for a while, and then Mara said, "You look a lot like your dad."

"Everyone tells me that," I said. Dad and I both had kind of bronze-colored hair and dark eyes. Mom and Star looked alike too, with blond hair and pale blue eyes.

"You live here all the time?"

"Yep, I'm a real conch. I was born here."

"What's a conch?"

"It's really a shellfish, but people who live on the Keys are called conchs."

"Do you go to school here?"

"We go to school up in Tavernier, about fifteen miles north of here. They have electricity for two or three hours in the morning. But when I go to high school next year, I'll have to board down in Key West. What grade are you in?"

"I'm going into tenth grade. I'll be fifteen next year."

"I'll be fifteen next year." I didn't tell her that my fourteenth birthday wouldn't be until December. I didn't want her to know I was only thirteen right now.

As we walked, I noticed that Mara was whistling a tune under her breath, so softly I could barely hear it. "That's the Atlantic Ocean on that side," I said, pointing to the dark-blue water to the east.

Mara stopped and looked out at the sea. "I never saw the Atlantic Ocean until today. Did you ever see so many shades of blue and green? It's like shiny ribbons spread across the sea."

I stopped too and followed her gaze. I'd never noticed that about the sea before. The shades of blue, turquoise, and emerald did look like ribbons all twisted together and laid across the water.

We began walking again. "How long will you be visiting your aunt?" I asked.

"Oh, I'm not visiting. I've come to live with her. And she's really my great-aunt."

I wondered why a girl about my age would come to live with Miss Edith, who looked at least a hundred years old.

Mara must have read my thoughts. "I lived in Pennsylvania with my dad, but last month he was killed in a coal-mine accident." She looked away.

"I'm real sorry to hear that," I said.

"Aunt Edith is my only relative now," she went on. "I've written to her off and on over the years, but we've never met. She's from Poland and so was my dad. When she heard that Daddy died, she sent me the money to come down and live with her here."

I wondered about Mara's mother. She hadn't mentioned her at all. "Is your mother living?"

"I don't have a mother," Mara answered abruptly.

No mother? That was a strange answer, but I

could tell that it was better not to ask any more. "You'll like it here," I said, trying to be cheerful. "Do you fish?"

"I never have. In Pennsylvania we lived near a coal mine, not the water."

"So that's how you know about the mules in the mines."

"Yes. Those mules are so smart. They know how to change the train rails for the coal carts by kicking the switches."

"Jewel seems to be a good mule—as mules go, I guess." I paused, shifted the suitcase from one hand to the other, and pointed to a two-story wooden building across the road. "That's the Matecumbe Hotel," I said. "It's not fancy like the hotels in Key West or Miami, but it looks real pretty with those new striped awnings, doesn't it?"

"Very pretty, but I've never stayed in a hotel."

"Me neither. People from up north come down here to fish in the winter. They stay at the hotel, unless, of course, they're rich enough to stay at the Millionaires Club near the water."

"No wonder people come down. It's like paradise here." Mara smiled, and her face lit up.

I laughed. "That's what folks call this place. Paradise. Actually, Islamorada means 'island home.'"

"Now it will be *my* island home." Mara looked up at me with a grin. "I'd like to learn to fish now that I'm here."

"I'll teach you," I said.

As we walked, not speaking for a while, I noticed Mara's soft whistling again. When we passed by the Robinsons' house, Ripper, their burly dog with bowed legs and a big head, barked viciously and pulled against his chain. Mara clutched my arm, and her eyes widened. "Can he get loose?"

"Don't worry, he's shackled up good. But he's strong and nasty. Don't ever go near him," I warned her.

We had approached Miss Edith's little gray shack. "This is your aunt's place," I said, setting the suitcase on the porch. We looked around, but there was no sign of her anywhere. The few chickens she kept clucked around our feet.

Mara knocked on the door. "Aunt Edith?" she called.

The door creaked open and Miss Edith stood

in the shadows. Except for a bright orange cobbler's apron, she was as pale as a ghost in the darkness of the room. Then I realized she was spattered with flour. "Oh my, oh my! You must be my dear Mara! I'm so forgetful! I was so busy cooking up *kolacki* and *pierniki* for you, I completely forgot the time! I can't believe I wasn't there to greet you! So foolish of me."

"It's all right, Aunt Edith. Jake brought me here."

Miss Edith reached out and gathered Mara into her arms. "Welcome, my little Mara!" she exclaimed. Miss Edith turned to me, wiped her pastry-covered fingers on her colorful apron, and stretched out her hand to me. "Thank you, Jake. You're such a good boy."

"You're welcome, Miss Edith," I said, carefully shaking her hand. The whole house smelled of good things to eat.

Once again, Edith Kraynanski took Mara into her arms. "I'm glad you've come to live with me, Mara."

"Thank you for sending for me, Aunt Edith," Mara said. "When Daddy died, I felt so alone and lost. I didn't know what to do or where to go." Mara's voice broke into a sob. "And then I got your letter and knew I still had someone in the world who cared what happened to me."

For a moment my own throat tightened. I couldn't even imagine what it must be like to lose your family and be alone in the world.

"It's all right, dear," Miss Edith said, stroking Mara's long hair. "This is your home now."

"And I have a new friend. Jake is going to teach me how to fish." Mara turned and smiled at me through her tears.

It made me feel good to see her smile—and to be called her friend.

I went over to Sharkey's after saying good-bye to Mara and Miss Edith. Jewel was tied up with a thick rope to a gumbo-limbo tree, while Rudy was checking out the landscape, sniffing and smelling every bush. Dad had gone on home, and Sharkey was trying to erect a rickety fence that had fallen down over the years.

"This thing's too old and rotted." He hurled the dilapidated wood into the brush. "I need something else to keep this mule confined. Though maybe Jewel will be okay and stick around once she knows this is home."

"If you tie Rudy up, Jewel would probably stay with him," I suggested.

"Humph!" He held a pail up to Jewel's nose and she pushed her head into the bucket. "Oats," he said. "Your dad stopped by the store on the way over here and brought some for me. I'll call the farmers' market in Homestead and ask them to send hay on next Tuesday's train."

I stood by, watching. It was getting late. I hoped Sharkey remembered that he'd offered to lend me his favorite fly for the contest tomorrow. He'd also given his word that he'd pay me for helping him today, but he hadn't mentioned it again.

Jewel roamed around on her long rope after she ate the oats, and she discovered a star-fruit tree with a couple of early fruits on the lower branches. "They're not ripe yet!" I exclaimed, as if Jewel knew the difference. She sniffed the fruits, and within a second she had neatly picked them off the branch and was eating them happily.

"She'll never go hungry," Sharkey said with a snort. "Looks like she can fend for herself."

"What about Rudy?"

"He can eat what I eat."

"We know he likes hot dogs." I suddenly remembered that I had paid for the frankfurter in Key West. So Sharkey owed me for that, too. Should I ask him about my pay? I kicked the dirt, not sure what to do. "I guess I better head home. Mom will have supper ready. And I'll need to get up early tomorrow for the fishing contest."

Sharkey nodded absently as I started up the path toward the road.

"Hey, Jake!" he called after me. "Come back here! Don't you want your pay?"

I turned around. "Sure! I almost forgot."

Sharkey pulled out his wad of money, sliced off three one-dollar bills, and handed them to me. "Not a bad day's wage, eh?"

Three dollars was a great day's wage. Dad talked a lot about the Depression; he said many folks in Florida only made seven dollars a month! Plus, I'd had the trip to Key West and, well, it was fun. Especially watching Sharkey at the auction. "Thanks, Sharkey," I said.

"Listen, kid," Sharkey continued, "you didn't even ask me for the money. That's no way to do business. You've got to speak up for yourself. Don't be afraid to ask for what's rightly yours."

"I . . . forgot," I lied again, gazing down at my feet.

"We both know you didn't forget." Sharkey

bent closer. "Now, if we're going to work together, you have to be honest with me. I won't bite." He put out his hand. "Deal?"

"Deal." I shook his hand, took a deep breath, and spoke right up. "You owe me a nickel for the hot dog."

Sharkey reached into his pocket. "You're right. I do." He gave me the coin. "Get over here early tomorrow, and we'll do a little fishing out in the flats. I'll take you to one of my secret places for bonefish. And once you catch a good-sized silver beauty with me, you'll become an honorary member of the Bonefish Brigade."

I was getting excited. The Bonefish Brigade was a group the famous author Zane Grey started when he came to fish on the Keys, and Sharkey had often been his guide. Fishing for the swift gray ghosts was fast becoming a popular sport.

"As I said, I'll let you use one of my favorite flies," Sharkey said. "We'll fish off my boat, so you don't need hip boots."

"I've never tried fly-fishing. I've caught a couple of small bonefish using shrimp."

Sharkey shrugged. "You can use shrimp if

you'd rather. No skin off my back," he muttered.

"No, no, the fly sounds good," I said quickly. "Thanks!"

During supper that night I told Mom and Dad about my trip to Key West, and how Sharkey bid on the mule. They laughed when they heard how he ended up with the dog, too.

"What's a mule?" Star asked.

"It's part horse, part donkey," Mom explained.

"What's its name?" Star sputtered, her mouth now full of spaghetti.

"Jewel," I answered.

"Can I have a ride on Jewel?" Star asked.

"No, you can't. Jewel's a working mule; she's not a pony," I told her.

"You're mean, Jake," she said with a pouty face.

Mom pulled Star over and wiped her face with a napkin. "Sharkey could use some help hauling in his boats and getting around with his bad leg. The mule might come in handy for him."

"Sharkey said he was glad you went with him today, Jake," Dad said.

"You know what? Even though he can be real

grouchy, I'm getting to like Sharkey!" I told them. "He's taking me fishing tomorrow morning."

"I need you to watch Star tomorrow morning," Mom said.

"Mom! Sharkey's going to teach me how to use his flies."

"Not tomorrow he's not," Mom stated with a frown. "You're watching Star."

"Mom, I can't! The fishing contest is tomorrow, and I need Sharkey's help to win." I glanced at Dad for reinforcement, but Mom had already given him a glare that meant, *Back me up here.*

Dad looked down at his plate and pushed the meatballs around. "Jake's already got plans with Sharkey, Louella," he finally said.

Mom's eyes narrowed. "I have to make pies and biscuits and sandwiches for the weekenders, Doug. You know it's hard to work on Saturdays with Star getting into things."

"Maybe Jake can take Star fishing with him," Dad suggested.

"I want to go fishing with Jake!" Star begged.

My heart sank. I'd go crazy with Star. She'd be pestering me every minute. "No, Dad! I watch Star all the time. Billy and Roy said I'll be a nursemaid when I grow up!"

"They should talk!" Mom said. "They have to watch Bessie, don't they?"

"But there are two of them, so they at least have some time to themselves." I turned to Dad again. "Dad, this is my chance to learn from Sharkey. Maybe someday I can be a guide for the millionaires, like he is."

"I want to go fishing too!" Star whimpered, her eyes filling up with tears.

"We'll work something out," Dad said, with a nod at Mom and a wink at me.

"Thanks, Dad," I said gratefully.

"There's nothing to work out," Mom said. "Jake watches Star tomorrow morning. That's it!"

Dad and Mom were staring each other down, and Star was crying. It was a good time for me to leave and keep my fingers crossed that Dad would win. I got up from the table, accidentally knocking a meatball on the floor as I went toward the kitchen. "Don't spill anything on my genuine American Oriental rug!" Mom yelled after me.

I grabbed the meatball and then deposited my

dishes in the sink with a loud clatter. "Why do I have to be stuck with Star all the time?" I muttered, loud enough to be heard over Star's howling. I went outside and let the door slam behind me, not stopping to put on my shoes.

I marched up the steep incline to the train tracks and headed toward town, still muttering and miserable. I knew I could win the contest tomorrow if I could just go fishing with Sharkey. But now everything would be ruined because I had to watch Star. Up the road, Ripper was barking fiercely at something. It seemed like that dog never stopped howling. "Shut up, you mutt!" I yelled. He snarled and barked even more viciously at my voice. Goose bumps prickled my arms and neck.

As I approached Miss Edith's house, Mara waved to me from the porch. "Jake!" she called. "Come down and visit!"

I stumbled down the embankment and slumped on the porch steps. Mara and Miss Edith were sitting in faded wooden rocking chairs. "Join us in some dessert," Miss Edith said. "There's a nice breeze tonight, and the mosquitoes are somewhere else for a change."

"Aunt Edith made these Polish *kruszczyki* today," Mara said, passing a plate of cookies.

"No, thanks. I'm not hungry," I said gloomily.

Mara handed me a glass of limeade. "We're out of ice until the iceman comes tomorrow, so it's a bit warm."

"Thanks," I said, taking the glass she offered.

"Is everything all right, Jake?" Miss Edith asked. "You were marching along the railroad bed like you were on a mission." She looked down at my bare feet. "No shoes, either."

"I was mad when I left the house and I forgot my shoes," I said.

"What's wrong?" Mara asked.

"I was planning to go bonefishing with Sharkey tomorrow. He was going to teach me to fish with his special flies. But now Mom wants me to watch Star."

"That's his little sister," Miss Edith explained to Mara. "She's a darling child."

"She's a pain in the neck, that's what she is!" I burst out. "My whole day will be spoiled. The kids are having the fishing contest tomorrow, and I'm going to have to miss it."

Mara and Miss Edith rocked silently in their chairs. Then Mara asked, "Aunt Edith, what are we doing tomorrow?"

"I had nothing planned, except to gather some eggs in the morning." Miss Edith sighed. "I would show you around the town, except my arthritis has been acting up lately. There's not much to see anyway. We live simply here, my dear."

Mara looked over at me. "Jake, I can watch Star while you go fishing."

"Oh wow! That'd be great," I said. "But Mara, I wasn't hinting ... I mean, I didn't expect you ..."

"Oh, I know," Mara said. "I'd enjoy watching Star."

I thought about the three dollars I got from Sharkey. "I'd be glad to pay you something."

"No. You don't need to do that," she said with that bright smile of hers. "But don't forget that you promised you'd teach me to fish sometime."

"I sure will!" I said, jumping up. "Why don't you walk down to my house with me, and we'll tell my folks."

"Do you need me here, Aunt Edith?" Mara asked.

"No, I'm fine, dear," Miss Edith said. "I'm enjoying myself sitting right here. It's not often we can do this and not be eaten alive by the mosquitoes."

Mara and I climbed back up the railroad bed and headed to my house. "Jake, look over there," she said, pointing to the sunset over the bay. "The sky and water look like a stained-glass window— all gold and red."

I looked out at the bay and stopped. "You're right. I never thought about it, but they do look like church windows." Mara seemed to notice everyday things in a different way.

We went into the store and up the stairs to the family kitchen. Mom was washing the dishes, and Star was sitting on Dad's knee with her book of poems. "Hello again, Mara," Dad said.

"This is Mara," I said to Mom.

Mom wiped off her soapy hand and held it out. "Welcome to Islamorada, Mara."

"Thank you, Mrs. Pitney," Mara said, shaking Mom's hand. "Jake has been very kind to me since I arrived."

"I heard that your papa died," Mom said. "I'm so sorry."

"Thank you." Mara replied.

"Mom, Mara said she'd watch Star tomorrow morning so I can go out fishing with Sharkey."

Mom frowned at me. "Did you ask Mara on her first day here to take over your responsibility?"

"Oh no, Mrs. Pitney," Mara assured her, "Jake didn't ask me. I offered to do it. I love children." She walked over to Star, who hid her face in Dad's chest. "Hello, Star. Would you like to visit me tomorrow?" Star shook her head and wouldn't look at Mara.

"Star," Dad said, "you're not being polite."

"Star's always shy with new people at first," said Mom.

Mara won't want to take care of Star if she won't even speak to her, I thought.

Mara took Star's book from Dad. "Hmm, *Wind and Stars and Bright Blue Skies.* This sounds like a nice book. Tomorrow we'll sit on my porch and I'll read it to you—or you can read it to me." She thumbed through the pages. "What sweet pictures and poems. Is this your favorite book?" Star turned her face away from Dad's chest and nodded at Mara.

"Tomorrow morning I'll come for you, and you can show me your favorite poem. Okay?"

"Okay," Star said.

"And I'll tell you my favorite poem, too."

Mom smiled at Mara. "This is so kind of you, Mara."

"I'm glad to help," Mara replied.

After I put on my shoes, Mara and I went back outside and headed toward town again. I noticed that a group of people had gathered near the packinghouse next to the train station.

"I wonder what's going on," I muttered. Mara and I picked up our pace to see what all the commotion was about. Veterans who worked on the highway were milling around Mr. Ashburn, Billy and Roy's dad. He was hollering and flailing his arms.

Next to him a wooden crate of tomatoes had tipped over and broken, scattering the red fruit everywhere. In the midst of it all stood Jewel, who was curiously sampling a tomato. Rudy sat nearby, watching.

Mr. Ashburn crowed at the top of his voice, "This crate was sealed and waiting right here for tomorrow's train!" He spun around at the group of veterans who had joined the skirmish. "Sealed tight!" he repeated accusingly. "This was no accident."

"No," Milt Barclay said, trying not to laugh. "It was downright thievery! I witnessed the whole thing."

"Who did this? Who vandalized this crate of tomatoes?" Mr. Ashburn asked.

"It was that thieving mule right there," Harry Webber called out, pointing to Jewel, who snorted, tossed her head, and spit out a squashed tomato.

It was obvious that she did not like tomatoes.

Mr. Ashburn looked over at Jewel, then scratched his head. "Where did this mule come from anyway? And whose dog is that?"

At that moment Sharkey appeared from the path across the road. He hobbled as fast as he could toward the crowd. "They're both mine!"

"Since when, Sharkey?" Mr. Ashburn demanded.

"Since today!" Sharkey's voice was defiant. He brandished his cane and everyone backed off as he made his way into the center of the hubbub. "What's going on?"

"Someone broke into one of my crates and spilled tomatoes all over the place. They're no good now—all smashed and ruined. They were going off to Homestead tomorrow to the farmers' market. All these tomatoes are a loss of good money and hard work! Don't you know there's a depression going on?"

"The mule did it!" a veteran called out.

"Now listen here," Sharkey said, taking hold of Jewel's bridle. "Even though Jewel here is the smartest mule in Florida, she wouldn't be likely to open a sealed tomato crate. Besides, it's too neatly broken for a mule to have done it. See? There are only two slats cracked. The scoundrel who did it neatly cracked two of the boards and then spilled the contents. Jewel simply took advantage of the situation and helped herself to a tomato." Sharkey whistled to Rudy, and without another word the three of them headed back across the road and into the woods.

Everyone was silent, then after a few moments Mr. Ashburn said, "When I find out which one of you men opened that crate, I'm complaining to your boss. The government sent you down to build a highway—not to play tricks on the locals!"

"We vets get blamed for everything around here," Harry Webber grunted.

"It was the mule," Milt Barclay insisted. "I saw it for myself. She and the dog were wandering around, and when they came to the tomato crate, that mule poked at it with her nose. Next thing she kicked the wooden slats and broke them open."

"Time will tell who's to blame," Mr. Ashburn said. "If that mule and dog cause more trouble around here, I'll run them out of town myself."

Mr. Ashburn righted the broken crate, and Mara and I began picking up the good tomatoes and putting them back inside.

"Thanks," Mr. Ashburn said to us. "Blaming a mule—huh! Those veterans are more trouble than they're worth."

But I had a strong feeling that Jewel really was the vandal that broke open the tomato crate.

It was getting dark as we headed back to Miss Edith's. "Thanks for watching Star tomorrow, Mara. I was excited when Sharkey said he'd fish with me, and I was just about ready to move out when Mom said I had to watch Star instead."

"Sharkey is . . . interesting," Mara said.

"He's lived here a long time in an old boxcar that was left over from the railroad. Folks know him and like him all right. But he can be unpredictable. He came chasing me off his land just yesterday, but then he hired me to help him today."

"Why'd he chase you off his property?"

"He thought I was digging up a turtle nest. He's so fussy about the sea turtles."

"He was protecting the nest?"

"Yes. And he fights off any animals that might disturb it. But he chases kids away all the time."

"Why would they be on the property to begin with?"

"They spy on him."

"Why on earth would they do that?"

"Because of the rumors . . ."

"What rumors?" Mara asked, slapping a mosquito.

"Sharkey used to be a wrecker. They're men who go out to shipwrecks to salvage cargo."

"So? That sounds like a respectable job."

"Wreckers sometimes find old shipwrecks with gold and don't tell the government, but just keep the gold for themselves."

"So you think Sharkey may have a stash of pirate gold?" Mara laughed.

I could feel my face redden. "Not *me*! I don't believe it," I said. "It's the other kids—Roy and Billy and . . ."

"If he has gold, why would he be living in a freight car?"

"I wondered about that myself," I said with a laugh.

We passed by the Robinsons' house, and Ripper began his loud growling and barking. "He scares me," Mara whispered.

When we reached Miss Edith's house, the

mosquitoes were out in full force. Miss Edith had shut the doors, and I could barely see the lantern light from inside, as the glass was thick with the buzzing pests.

"I hope you'll have a good time with Sharkey tomorrow," Mara said, reaching for the latch.

I swatted at the mosquitoes. "It won't be fun. Sharkey is probably going to be cranky. But he'll help me bag a bonefish."

"Jake, you just told me Sharkey protects the turtle nests, didn't you?"

"Well, yeah," I said. "He does."

"Haven't you noticed how gently Sharkey strokes Jewel and Rudy? And how he smiles at them?"

"Yeah, he does love animals," I agreed. "Just not kids."

"But Jake—why would he take you fishing if he doesn't like kids?" She opened the door quickly and ducked inside.

Mara arrived at our house early on Saturday morning, and Mom insisted she join us for a bacon and eggs breakfast.

"Aunt Edith's favorite laying hen has disappeared," Mara told us. "It looks like there was a huge scuffle around the nests. Feathers were scattered everywhere, and the other hens were frightened. We searched around but couldn't find Henny Penny, so there were no eggs this morning."

"Well, enjoy these eggs then," Mom said as she passed the gravy for the biscuits. "How long do you plan to stay here in Islamorada?"

"Forever, I guess," Mara answered. "I have nowhere else to go."

"It must be hard to leave your home up north. What about your mother?"

I stopped eating and waited to hear Mara's answer.

"My mother . . . she's gone too."

"Oh, how sad!" Mom continued. "When did she pass on?"

At that moment Star, still in her pajamas, ran from her bedroom and climbed into Mara's lap. "Can I go to your house? Shall I get my book?" she asked eagerly.

Mara smiled down at Star. "First tell me where you got your name."

"My name is Estelle. That means star. I'd rather be called Star." She began to sing loudly, "Twinkle, twinkle, little star . . ."

"You're a star, all right," Mara told her.

"She's not at all bashful with you today," Mom said, seeming to forget the question she had asked about Mara's mother. I was curious to know the answer and was annoyed with Star's interruption.

"I'd better get over to Sharkey's," I said, getting up.

"When you're finished, go straight over to Miss Edith's and get Star. There's no need for Mara to be watching her once you're back," Mom said.

"I will," I promised, with a smile and a nod at Mara.

"Let me take a look at your gear," Dad said. We headed downstairs to the store. In the back room our fishing poles leaned against the wall. My father looked over my rod and reel, then handed his best rod to me. "Use this instead. It will work better with a fly." He showed me how to work the reel and the thumb latch that controlled the release of the line.

"Thanks, Dad," I said, gathering the rest of my gear. "I'll be back after the contest."

"Catch a good one," he said. "And win that contest!"

I walked as fast as I could while juggling the rod, a tackle box, and a bucket and slapping the mosquitoes that buzzed around me. When I finally got to Sharkey's place, I was sweaty and breathless.

Sharkey had his flat-bottomed guide boat fastened to the rickety dock and was filling the engine with gas from a red metal can. Jewel was tied to a tree with a long, heavy rope, and Sharkey had set up a run for Rudy with a pulley so he could walk around. But right now they were both lying on the ground, Jewel with her long legs curled under her, and Rudy with his head on his paws. When Rudy saw me, he sat up and barked a few times.

"It's okay, Rudy," I said, patting him. He wagged his silky tail and lay down again.

Sharkey looked up when he heard the bark. "I hope those animals will behave themselves while we're gone," he said crossly.

I headed down to the dock. "How did they get away last night?"

"Jewel unhitched the knot on that tether I used to tie her up."

"How did she do that?"

"With her teeth. Completely unfastened the rope." Sharkey took a rag and wiped up some gasoline that had spilled around the engine and can. "That mule is too smart for her own good. I've double-knotted the rope for now. I'm going to have you help me put up a fence and gate next week. I can't have those two running off and bothering people."

I wanted to fish with Sharkey more than anything, but now I wondered if he would rather stay home and watch his animals. "Maybe we shouldn't go ...," I began.

"What? Not go fishing? These two misfits aren't going to rule my life. Come on! Hop into this tub and let's go." I climbed in, and he pulled the rope starter a few times. The outboard motor coughed and then began to purr.

I freed the bow and stern lines and pushed us off.

"We'll go to one of my favorite feeding grounds," Sharkey said. "That way you won't have to entrust me with your secret fishing place." I was curious to see where he would take me.

We headed out into the flats between several small islands on the bay side. The sun was getting higher in the sky, and it was already sweltering. A mullet jumped to catch the mosquitoes that hovered over the still water.

After a mile or so we came to a shallow inlet near a stretch of mangroves. "There's a channel parallel to this flat," Sharkey said. "See how the water is moving toward the bay? Bonefish like to feed back and forth through here."

Sharkey turned the motor off, and we drifted silently in the shallows where fish swam among the clusters of mangroves. He stood on a platform above the stern so he could get a better view of the flats and the fish below. From my seat I could see flashes of silver, and the sharp tails of a school of bonefish as they broke the surface and bent down to feed. *This must be one of Sharkey's best fishing spots.*

Sharkey took a long pole, put it into the mud, and pushed us quietly toward the bonefish. A few of the tails disappeared as we came closer. "Here, clip my jigger bug onto your leader," Sharkey whispered. He handed me a lure that looked like a strange insect with pink squiggly legs and hooks on both ends.

"I thought you said I could use one of your flies," I said as I snapped the lure in place on Dad's rod.

"I did. Flies work. But you need to use a more delicate stroke. I think the lure will work better for a beginner."

"I'm not a beginner," I protested. "I fish all the time."

"If you're such an expert, use your own bait."

Here he goes again, I thought. *Sharkey, King of the Old Cranks.* But I didn't say a word. Instead I stood on the bow and cast the line. The pink lure with its squiggly legs landed with a plop, and all the tails of the bonefish disappeared.

"Look at the splash you made! That's enough to scare all the fish from here to Cuba! Here, let me show you." Sharkey came up by me and took the rod. "You need to flex your wrist, not your whole arm, when you cast. And don't let out too much line." He adjusted the reel and then cast. This time the lure landed with hardly a ripple. He handed the rod to me. "Try it again."

After several attempts, I was able to flip the lure into the water the way a bug or fly might land.

As we waited for the fish to bite, I thought about Mara and what she'd said the night before about Sharkey. "Sharkey," I whispered. "When we started out for Key West, had you planned to buy a mule? Was it really because of your bad leg?"

"No," Sharkey answered. "Never came to my mind—until I saw her. I used to work with mules when the railroad was going up, and in the war, too. I like them. They've had a raw deal. People joke about them and make fun of them, but they're the salt of the earth—hardworking and tough—and gentle if they're treated right."

A lot like Sharkey himself, I thought.

"So how come you bought Jewel?"

"Didn't you hear the owner saying he would put her down? I couldn't let that happen. Besides, I know a good mule when I see one." Sharkey put his finger to his lips. "Now stop yapping or you'll never catch a fish."

We waited quietly, and before long the tails appeared again among the mangroves in the shallow water. In the sky a flock of bright pink spoonbills fluttered, their reflections mirrored on the surface. Other birds chirped among the branches of the mangroves, while I cast over and over again. The sun was straight above us now. It was close to noon and time to take our catches to Ashburn's wharf. And I didn't have a fish!

Suddenly I felt a tug, as a fish took off like a shot with my line. "I've got one!" I shouted to Sharkey.

"Bring him in slowly," Sharkey directed. "Let him play with it a little."

I did as he said. The fish sped off; then gently I reeled him back. I could see the glitter of silver as the fish fought against the line. Little by little I brought him closer to the boat. Sharkey grabbed a net and put it under the wriggling fish. "Nice one!" he exclaimed, pulling up the net and handing it to me. "Here, you unhook him. It's your fish."

Gently I pulled the hook from its mouth and then placed the fish in a bucket of seawater.

"Let's take him back to the Ashburns' wharf right away," I said. "That's where the contest is being held. I'll bet I'm the only one with a bonefish!"

Sharkey started the engine, and we put-putted to the inlets that led to the Atlantic side then up toward the Ashburns' place. I could see a dozen or so kids fishing off their pier or in nearby rowboats. Even Bessie was fishing. This time, at least, I didn't have Star hanging around with me.

"Hey, Jake!" Roy yelled, and waved us in. He held up a large sea bass for me to see.

Sharkey cut the engine, and we drifted right up to the dock. I grabbed the bonefish out of the pail and held it up high by the gills. "How's this for a catch?" I yelled. The kids' mouths dropped open. "We didn't weigh it yet, but I'll betcha no one else got a bonefish."

There was some muttering among the kids, and then Billy yelled out, "Not fair! You had Sharkey helping you."

Several other kids chimed in. "Not fair!"

"You're disqualified!" Roy called.

Disqualified?" I yelled, once I was able to speak. "You're the ones not being fair!"

"But you had a guide!" Roy hollered. "None of us has a guide."

I stood in the boat and waved my fish. "You weren't fishing for bonefish! Whenever the millionaires fish for their tournaments, they always have a guide, and they're never disqualified!"

"Forget it, Jake," Billy yelled. "Looks like we've got the winner here with this snook." He motioned to another kid on the pier who was reeling in a good-size fish.

"Come on," Sharkey said, starting up the engine.

I put the fish back in the bucket. It was listless now, and I hoped it wouldn't die. "We fished all morning, and now they tell me I'm disqualified," I sputtered. As we made our way through the coves to the other side of the key, I fumed at Billy and Roy and the others. "They were jealous of my bonefish! That's why they banded together to make my fish ineligible."

I released the fish back into the bay and watched it shimmer, circle, and then swim out of sight. Sharkey patted my shoulder and said, "Don't let the kids bother you."

"The kids are green-eyed with envy that I went to Key West with you and that you were my guide."

"Why would they be envious?"

"You're kind of famous, Sharkey. They think you might be a pirate and have a treasure hidden somewhere."

"Me? A pirate with a treasure?" Sharkey laughed. "If I had a treasure, would I be living in that old boxcar? I'd *be* one of the millionaires, instead of working for them."

"But you were a wrecker, weren't you?"

"That's true," Sharkey said.

"What kind of things did you salvage when you were a wrecker, then?" I asked.

"I recovered whatever goods were on board, providing they were still salvageable—things like bales of cotton, sugar, and bolts of cloth, depending on how much water got to them. Many of the ships weren't totally underwater. Some were modern ships stranded on rocks or sinking from storms. We wreckers reclaimed what we could for the insurance companies, but we had to move fast before the material was destroyed by salt water." Sharkey wiped the sweat off his forehead with his sleeve. "The work was treacherous, not just from the depth of the water or the dangers in the ship itself, but because if we didn't get to the goods quick enough, fish or rice or other things would rot and become poisonous. Some divers have gone blind from the rotting materials."

"So no pirate treasure?" I said, disappointed.

Sharkey grinned as he steered the boat toward his place. "I came across some old silver and gold coins on the bottom of the sea a few times. I sold most of them to a jewelry shop owner who made them into necklaces." Sharkey opened his shirt. At last I was going to get a good look at what hung from the heavy gold chain around his neck. He held out the shining coin. "This is from a Spanish shipwreck back in the sixteen hundreds."

I looked closer and could see a cross and an inscription in a language I guessed to be Spanish. "Wow! That's really swell, Sharkey. Do you think there are more old treasures still out there?"

"Of course there are, but I've stopped looking for them. I do have a few doubloons left, though. Remind me to show you sometime."

We were now pulling into the cove where Sharkey lived. "Well, I'll be danged," Sharkey said as we came up to the wharf. "Look at Jewel. She's untied her rope again!"

Sure enough, Jewel was standing next to Rudy, who was still hitched up on his run. "Jewel untied her own knots, but couldn't undo Rudy's, I guess." We both laughed.

"That mule is as smart as any person on this island," Sharkey said as we got out of the boat. I was about to head home when he said, "I suppose you'll be going to church tomorrow morning." When I nodded, he looked disappointed. "Well, I can wait until Monday—if you can help me, that is. I want to see about putting up an enclosure for Jewel, and we'll need a whole day to do it. I spoke to Pete Lowery from Tavernier last night. He just took down a fence, and he's bringing the good stuff to me by boat tomorrow. He's not charging me a cent, either."

"Maybe I can skip church tomorrow."

"Ask your folks. If not, come by Monday and I'll put you to work."

"Thanks for fishing with me, Sharkey."

"Sorry you didn't win the contest," he said. "But there will be other fishing tournaments you can enter. Real ones." He went over to Jewel and patted her neck. When she nuzzled him, he pulled a berry from the sea-grape tree and offered it to her. She sniffed it, then ate it in one gulp.

As I went out the dirt path to the road, I was still mad at Roy and Billy, though I tried to convince myself that it didn't matter. Their contest was just kid stuff. As Sharkey said, there'd be other, *real* fishing tournaments.

When I arrived at Miss Edith's, Mara and Star were on the front porch, stretched out in a hammock that hung from the rafters and was enclosed with mosquito netting. Mara sat up and crept out from the netting, her finger to her lips. "Star's asleep," she whispered. Star stirred a little and then put her thumb in her mouth. "Did you catch a bonefish? Did you win the contest?" Mara asked.

I sat on a chair by the hammock and told her about my morning. "I'm really mad at Roy and Billy," I said, whacking a mosquito. "They changed the rules when they saw that I had bagged a nice bonefish."

"That's too bad," she said. "Aunt Edith is upset today too. She discovered what happened to Henny Penny. Turns out some animal came and took the poor little thing away."

"Probably a raccoon," I said.

"I don't know about that," Miss Edith said, coming onto the porch. "The tracks I saw weren't a raccoon's. They were a dog's." She motioned to me to follow her.

I followed Miss Edith into the yard and beyond the overhanging sea-grape trees. She pointed to the soft, damp earth where the feathers had been scattered. I bent over and immediately recognized the large paw prints I had seen at Sharkey's. "Those are panther tracks," I told her.

"Nonsense! We don't have a panther around here. It's a dog, Jake."

"Whose dog?" I asked.

"I don't know. But I saw that huge mongrel of Sharkey's running around with the mule yesterday."

"It couldn't be Rudy," I said. "He's a friendly dog. He wouldn't hurt anything."

Miss Edith shook her head. "Well, I never had a problem before."

"We've seen panther tracks over at Sharkey's, too."

"That's what you think you saw. But they were really from that new dog!" she insisted.

"I saw those paw marks before Rudy was even in town," I argued. "Besides, these are much bigger than what Rudy would make." I knelt down and looked closely at the prints. "There are no signs of claws, Miss Edith. Sharkey and I were discussing it just the other day. If it were a dog, there'd be imprints of its nails. A panther is a cat and has retractable claws."

"There are no panthers this far down in the Keys," Miss Edith argued. "I'm sorry, Jake, but I think that dog and mule are going to be trouble-makers. If I find another missing chicken, I'm complaining to the authorities." She shoved both hands deep into the pockets of her orange apron and abruptly turned away, firmly ending the discussion.

The authorities she spoke of were probably the Audubon rangers. They showed up frequently looking for bird poachers. Anyone caught trapping or hurting birds could get into big trouble—and chickens were birds, weren't they?

I knew Miss Edith was upset because she'd lost her favorite hen, but I sure hoped she wouldn't make trouble for Rudy and Jewel!

When we got back to the porch, Star was waking up, and her eyes were heavy with sleep. She pushed aside the netting and outstretched her arms. "Jake!" I went over and gave her a hug.

"She talks about you all the time," Mara told me as she sat on the hammock next to Star. "Jake this and Jake that."

I shrugged and rolled my eyes. "She's my shadow."

"I'm not your shadow, Jake," Star said.

"Twinkle, twinkle, little Star," I teased, "now I know just what you are. You're my shadow chasing me. Why won't you ever let me be?"

"Don't say that!" Star whined, her mouth quivering.

"Why, Jake. You're a poet and didn't even know

it!" Mara winked at Star and patted her hand. "Star showed me her favorite poems today."

"That's nice," I responded. I knew all of Star's favorite poems by heart, having read them dozens of times.

"Mara writes poems," Star said.

Mara smiled and looked away. "They're not very good, but I like to write them. They . . . help me sort things out in my head."

"Read them to Jake," Star blurted. "Jake likes poems. Don't you, Jake?"

"Um, well, I only read Star's book of verses. But I'd like to hear *your* poems, Mara."

"Maybe sometime," she said.

After thanking her again, I took Star's hand and we headed home. Star babbled all the way. "Mara is so nice. She brushed my hair, and it didn't hurt like when you do it, Jake," she said in a disapproving manner.

"Boys aren't supposed to brush girls' hair."

"Why not?"

"I don't know. They just aren't, that's all."

"Mara wrote a poem about snow. She played in the snow back home, Jake. She said snow is cold.

And it's pretty and clean." Star chattered on and on like a squirrel. "I want to see snow someday. Why doesn't it snow here?"

"It's too hot here to snow," I told her.

"I have stones in my shoes." Star sat down on the road. I unbuckled her sandals one at a time, shook out the dirt, and put them back on her feet again.

"Come on, Star. Don't bellyache all the time." I pulled her up with a tug. After hearing Miss Edith's complaints about Jewel and Rudy, I wanted to help Sharkey get a fence up right away, and that meant skipping church. Mom would give me a hard time, I was sure of that.

And I was right. When I got home Mom was in the upstairs kitchen paring potatoes. "Don't you dare skip church!" she exclaimed when I told her about my plan to work with Sharkey on Sunday. "I can't imagine that Sharkey would suggest such a thing!" She eyed me suspiciously. "Or was it your idea?"

"Sharkey didn't ask me to skip church. But I know he needs help."

Mom had her hands on her hips, which meant

she was ready for an argument, when Dad came into the living room. "Anything the matter?" He looked at me and then at Mom.

"Jake wants to skip church tomorrow and help Sharkey." She stared at Dad's feet and snapped, "Take off those dirty shoes! You're soiling my genuine American Oriental rug!"

Dad sighed, sat in a chair, and removed his shoes. "Sharkey's leg has been bad recently, and he needs help. You know Sharkey's a good man, Lou."

"That's not the point," Mom said. "Jake should not miss church."

"Why does Sharkey need you tomorrow?" Dad asked me.

"Sharkey needs to make a corral for Jewel and Rudy. The two of them keep getting away, and folks are getting mad. Now Miss Edith is blaming Rudy for killing Henny Penny."

Mom shook her head. "Sharkey brought trouble upon himself with those animals."

"It wasn't Rudy that killed the hen—it was a panther," I said. "If Sharkey can fence Rudy and Jewel in a pen, then they won't get blamed for everything."

"Sharkey's already been into the store buying bags of cement for a fence," Dad said. "Oh, let Jake go help, Lou."

Mom kept her hands on her hips. "No!" she said to Dad. "Jake needs to go to church."

"Sometimes helping your neighbor is just as important as going to church. Maybe even more important," Dad answered.

With a sigh, Mom threw up her hands in defeat and went back to slicing potatoes.

That night everyone except Star was quiet at the dinner table, but after a while Dad got Mom to smile again. No matter what the situation, Dad could always make Mom smile.

I woke up Sunday morning to the deep clanging of the bell that hung in the steeple of the Methodist Church. It was a reassuring sound that echoed throughout our little town. The church, a prim white building, stood on the shore, next to the town graveyard. Boats from other islands arrived on Sunday mornings so people could attend services at our church, which was the only one for miles around.

Mom was already up and dressed and brushing Star's long hair when I came into the kitchen. "Ow!" Star whined as Mom came upon a knot. "Mara doesn't hurt me when she brushes my hair!"

Mom sighed. "I'm going to cut your hair short like Bessie's. I can't go through this every day."

"Will Bessie be at Sunday school?" Star asked.

"Of course. The Ashburns are *always* there," Mom said with a meaningful look at me. "There are biscuits and sea-grape jelly on the table, Jake. Help yourself. But eat in the kitchen. I don't want—"

"Grape jelly on your rug," I filled in.

"It's the finest thing in this house—the only valuable thing I have," Mom said in that suffering voice she used whenever she felt put-upon. "And I'm still upset you're not attending Sunday services with us today."

"It's just this one Sunday, Mom," I said. "Sharkey needs help."

As I headed up the road, I was surprised to see Mara smiling and waving to me from her porch. She was dressed for church, wearing a flowered dress that looked freshly starched and ironed. Her dark red hair was curly this morning, and a pale-green headband held it back from her face. "Hi, Jake!" she called eagerly as she ran up the embankment to the road. "Are you going to church?"

"Not today," I answered.

Mara smile faded. "I was hoping you'd be there. I thought we might have a picnic afterward. But I guess you'll be busy."

"I'm going to help Sharkey today. But I'll probably be starving by one o'clock or so."

She grinned. "Come to my house around one. We can have a picnic down by the water."

"Okay!" I agreed.

At that moment a horse-drawn cart came rumbling onto the road. No, not horse-drawn, I realized. It was *mule*-drawn! Jewel was harnessed to Sharkey's wagon, which was loaded up with fencing. Sharkey walked in front, leading Jewel with a rope tether, and trotting in front of them were Rudy and Ginger.

"Looks like a circus!" Mara said with a laugh.

"Hey, Jake!" Sharkey yelled when he came closer. "Since you're not dressed for church, I can use some help over at my place."

"I'm coming!" I called back, and turning to Mara, I explained, "Sharkey's going to build a corral for Jewel and Rudy today."

"Oh, good! Then Aunt Edith won't be able to blame Rudy for taking her hens. But do you really think there's a panther around these parts?"

"I sure do. Panthers will come right up on the porch if they smell meat cooking in a kitchen." This had never actually happened to anybody I knew, but I'd heard the stories, and Mara listened intently to my every word.

"Really?"

"Yes. Just ask Miss Edith. I'm sure she knows those stories."

Mara's eyes widened. "Oh, my. I wouldn't know what to do if I came across a panther."

"Anyone could be in danger, especially if the cat is hungry," I warned her. "So keep on the watch!"

"Oh," Mara gasped, clapping her hand over her mouth. "That is scary!"

I was laying it on thick. I had never heard of a panther hurting anyone, but it sounded exciting.

"Come on, Jake!" Sharkey yelled. He and his

troupe were way up the road and heading onto the path that led to his place.

"I'm coming!" Turning to Mara, I clawed the air near her face. "Grrrr! Watch out for panthers, Mara," I growled.

Mara laughed. "Stop teasing me!" she scolded.

"You don't need to worry. You'll probably never see one!" I called out as I left.

I ran up the road to catch up with Sharkey and passed through the shade from the overhanging trees. *Could a panther be lurking in those dark shadows?* I wondered.

That morning Sharkey and I dug postholes around an area next to his house. It wasn't very big, but it would give Jewel a place to move around and stay out of trouble. Rudy sniffed and checked out the holes we had dug. Jewel, who stood nearby, constantly switched her tail and blinked her eyes to rid them of flies. Sharkey stopped occasionally to wipe Jewel's eyes and face with some kind of ointment that would repel the flies. I couldn't help but notice how gentle he was with her.

Sharkey picked up his shovel and dug once again into the dirt. "Did you see Jewel pulling that wagon? She knew just what to do as soon as I hitched her up."

"She's strong, hauling that cart full of timber so easily," I agreed, laughing. "Of course, you wouldn't have needed a cart full of timber if you hadn't bought the mule."

Sharkey smacked me in the seat of my pants with his shovel. "Get to work!" he ordered in his gruff voice.

After we finished digging the holes, we poured wet cement into them and set the posts into the concrete. "Let's take a break until the cement dries," Sharkey said. He stood back and looked at our work. "This plot of land will be fine. There's enough room for Jewel and Rudy to roam around."

"And still stay in one place!" I added. "There's a panther prowling near the town. It killed one of Miss Edith's chickens, but she thinks Rudy and Jewel are responsible."

"A panther must be very hungry to come that near to town."

"That's why she's so sure Rudy killed her hen. But I saw the tracks, and they were like the ones we saw here."

Sharkey took the shovels and carried them to the lean-to shed where he kept his tools. "They won't blame my animals once they're confined to the corral," he said. "Miss Edith should get her chickens contained in a safe place. Raccoons eat chickens too. I'm surprised she hasn't lost birds before this."

"I'll tell her. I'm going over there now for a picnic while the posts are setting."

When I arrived, Mara was waiting on the porch with a picnic basket in her lap. Her aunt sat in the rocking chair.

"Did you hear the latest, Jake?" Miss Edith asked. "Mike Robinson's dog, Ripper, was killed last night. To be truthful, I lived in fear of that dog, and I hated its constant yowling, but I wouldn't have wished such a horrible death on any beast."

I went up onto the porch. "What happened to it?" I asked.

"The Robinsons were up in Tavernier for the night and left Ripper chained as usual. I heard barking, but of course I didn't pay any attention, because that dog never stops. Well, last night the only thing different was that the barks were mingled with a few yelps, but I wasn't going near that dog to see if anything was wrong. When the barking stopped, I forgot about it."

"This morning the Robinsons found the dog dead in their yard—still chained," Mara said.

"What killed it?" I was afraid to hear the answer.

"The Robinsons blame Sharkey's dog, and they're fit to be tied, Jake!" Miss Edith exclaimed. "I'm sure he killed Henny Penny, too."

"I don't believe it was Rudy. He's too smart to get into a fight with Ripper. Rudy would have lost the fight. And Rudy's not mean. He hasn't chased any of the chickens, has he?"

"Well, no," Miss Edith admitted. "Actually, I've only seen him once or twice, heading down to the Ashburns' house."

"That's because Rudy has become acquainted with their dog, Ginger," I said. "They play together. Ginger comes up and visits Rudy at Sharkey's place, too."

"I'm sorry, Jake, but I can't afford to lose any more chickens. If I catch that dog on my property, I'll have to call the Audubon."

"Don't worry, Miss Edith," I said. "Sharkey's building a corral for Jewel and Rudy today. He says you should think about getting a house for the chickens to keep them safe from other predators, though."

"I'm telling you, no panther has ever prowled around here in all the years I've lived in this house," she said.

I was about to argue when Mara nodded toward the door. "Let's go," she whispered.

We took a path that led to the waterfront, passing under thick branches of trees. I stopped by the trunk of a gumbo-limbo and pointed to the smooth bark, which was scarred with scratches. "Look at this," I said.

"What do you suppose made those claw marks?" Mara said.

"Rudy, of course. He loves to climb trees!" I said sarcastically.

Our worries about the mysterious scratches diminished when we reached the clearing near the church and cemetery. It was beautiful with the bright sky and shining water.

The church service had been over for a while, and it was quiet along the waterfront. We went to the wharf, took off our shoes, and dangled our feet in the warm water. "Watch out for sharks," I said. "Your toes make good shark bait."

Mara pulled her feet in, and when I laughed, she poked me. "There you go again. I never know when you're kidding."

She pointed to the Ashburns' wharf down the shoreline. "What is that enclosure they have under their dock?"

"That's a kraal," I answered. "When they capture big turtles, they put them under there until they're ready to eat them. Sort of like a corral for turtles."

"I see. Kraal. Corral."

"When we have a big cookout here on the island, someone usually cooks up a turtle for soup."

"Kind of sad for the poor turtles," Mara said.

We ate tuna sandwiches with slices of tomato and then delicious twisted pastries sprinkled with cinnamon sugar. "These are *pierniki,*" Mara told me. "Polish cookies."

"Miss Edith makes great Polish food that she brings over to us sometimes. We look forward to her *golabki* and *babka*." I knew the Polish names for the cabbage rolls and cake that Miss Edith shared with us, and I wanted to show off to Mara.

"Many of the coal miners are of Polish descent," Mara explained. "And there are miners from Wales and Ireland, too."

She and I shared a small pineapple that Mara had cut into pieces. "Aunt Edith has her own little pineapple garden. Isn't that amazing? I didn't know they even grew in North America." She wiped the juice from her chin with a napkin.

"What kinds of fruit grow in Pennsylvania?" I asked.

"Strawberries and blueberries in the summer, and apples in the fall." She sighed. "I miss Pennsylvania—well, mostly I miss my daddy. I can't believe he's gone." Mara was quiet for a long moment. Then she said, "I don't miss the coal mines, though. There's nothing pretty about coal mines—except after a snowfall. That's when the fresh snow covers the black culm banks, and everything is white and clean."

"What are culm banks?"

"They're mounds of slate and pieces of unusable coal that are just left there once they've been picked over," she explained. "They're hideous—

except when the snow covers them. Then we go sledding on them."

"Star said you wrote a poem about the snow."

"It's very short. Would you like to hear it?"

"Sure."

Mara cleared her throat and closed her eyes.

Silent snow covers yesterdays.
For a moment, the past disappears.
How long, this shining, new place?
Only for a day.

She opened her eyes and smiled tentatively.

"Is that it?" I realized too late that this was a stupid thing for me to ask.

"Yes, that's it." She turned and gazed out to sea.

"I—I meant . . . it's short."

"I told you it was short."

"I like it, Mara. I just need you to explain it."

"If you need an explanation, you will never understand."

"Mara, I've never seen snow. So I need to . . . think about it. Would you say it again?" I pleaded. "Please?"

"No, Jake. Forget it."

We sat silently, the only sounds the buzzing of bees and the splashing of small waves against the dock.

"Mara, aren't poems supposed to rhyme?" I asked.

"No! Not all poems rhyme." Then she turned to me. "It's okay, Jake. You don't understand poetry, just as I don't understand . . . fishing."

"Please tell me the poem again. *Please.*"

Mara recited the verse once more, and I realized that her poem was something like a riddle.

After I thought about it for a few minutes, I said, "Your poem is kind of sad, as if good things happen only for a little while."

"That's it, Jake. It's about the fresh snow and how it covers the black, ugly culm banks. Then the snow melts, and everything goes back to the way it was. Nothing has really changed after all." She looked out at the sea again as if something were out there. I looked too, but there was only the sea and the sky.

Later, as we put our trash in the picnic basket to take home, Mara said, "Have you seen your mother since she got home from church?" I shook my head. "Then you haven't heard. I'm going to be looking after Star and Bessie three mornings a week. It gives your mom and Mrs. Ashburn the mornings free to do things, and it will be a break for you boys."

This was great news. Mom—or more likely Dad—was actually doing something about my babysitting complaints!

"When do you start?"

"I thought I'd take them both for a little walk this afternoon, just to get them used to the idea." We gathered our things and headed up the path toward Miss Edith's house. "We can play hide-and-seek, and pick berries or something."

"Star will love it," I told her.

After walking Mara home, I headed back to Sharkey's. First thing I told him was about the Robinsons' dog.

"I'll bet Ripper put up one heck of a fight," Sharkey said. "Was he eaten?"

"I don't know. Yuck!"

"Usually a panther will bury its kill to hide it from other animals; then it'll go back later to eat it again. But with Ripper being chained up, the panther wouldn't have been able to drag him away."

"The bad news is that Miss Edith is sure it was Rudy who did it."

Sharkey shook his head. "Ridiculous."

The cement we had poured earlier had hardened in the hot sun, and we were ready to put the fence together. The rails were laid out on the ground. Once they were put into place, the post-and-rail fence would be about five feet high.

"Do you suppose Jewel could jump the fence once you get it up?" I asked.

"Of course not!" Sharkey barked. "She couldn't jump that high without more running space."

"The fence won't keep Rudy in," I said. "He'll

wriggle under the rails and get out whenever he wants."

"It doesn't matter about Rudy," Sharkey said. "Rudy won't leave without Jewel, and Jewel will be stuck in the corral."

"Miss Edith says she's seen him heading down to see Ginger."

"How often did he do that? Once? Twice?" Sharkey frowned at me from under the broad rim of his hat. "Don't be such a wet blanket, Jake. Pete Lowery brought this fence all the way from Tavernier, and by golly, it's going to work or I'll drop dead trying."

By late afternoon we had the rails hitched up to the posts. One section was set up as a gate with a latch. A cone-shaped wooden pin fit into the shaft to lock the gate. Sharkey tried it several times. "No way this gate can open by itself," he said. Jewel was already in the center of the corral. "She's in here to stay." He seemed pleased.

Meanwhile Rudy had burrowed himself under the bottom rail. He stood outside the fence and paced back and forth, barking at Jewel, who acted troubled. Her long ears were thrust out in different directions. She trotted to where Rudy waited, and made strange snorts—a mixture of a horse's whinny and a donkey's bray.

"Too bad, Jewel," Sharkey said. "You're stuck in there, so settle down."

The mule walked around the enclosure, slowly circling. Suddenly, like an awkward dancer, Jewel bounded over the top rail, all four of her hooves easily clearing it. She landed next to Rudy, who was waiting with his tail waving like a flag in the breeze.

Sharkey and I stood there in our sweaty clothes, covered with dirt and cement dust, and blinked in astonishment. We'd spent the whole day erecting that fence. Now we realized it would never hold a mule that was able to leap over a five-foot rail from a standing position!

"I'll be danged!" Sharkey grabbed his hat and threw it on the ground. "I saw another mule high-jump like that once, but I never dreamed Jewel could do it! This corral won't be much good for holding *this* mule."

"Well, it is a nice-looking corral, Sharkey," I said, trying to look on the bright side.

Rudy trotted over to Sharkey as if to say,

What's the next job on the agenda? He lapped at Sharkey's hand, and his whole body wagged as Sharkey petted him. Sharkey bent down, and Rudy licked his face and beard.

Meanwhile Jewel had meandered to a seagrape tree whose grape clusters had become ripe. Some had fallen onto the ground, and she was gobbling them up contentedly.

Sharkey picked up his hat and dusted it off. "I guess I'll just have to get more timber and add another couple of rungs to the fence. All we need is a few more rails and Jewel won't get out that easily again."

When I returned home I told Mom and Dad all about my day building the fence. "So Jewel high-jumped the corral," Mom said, laughing.

About then we heard a loud knocking on the store door downstairs. "Who can that be on a Sunday night?" Dad muttered. He went down and I could hear Sharkey's anxious voice.

I flew to the stairway with Mom right behind me. "They're gone again, Doug," Sharkey was saying. "I went into my house for two minutes and they both disappeared."

"We haven't seen either of them," Dad said.

"I'll help you look," I offered, and went to put on my shoes.

"Yes, go with him, Jake," Mom called. "And while you're at it, bring Star home from Mara's. She went over there with Bessie to visit Mara for a while. Supper will be ready soon."

"I've already checked up by the train station, so now I'll head toward the church and cemetery," Sharkey explained. "I'll check with the Ashburns, too. Meanwhile you go down to the shore by way of Miss Edith's place."

Miss Edith was inside when I got there. Smoke was curling up from the chimney, and I could smell onions and cabbage cooking. I hated to inform Miss Edith that the mule and dog were loose again. She was upset when I asked her if she'd seen the two runaways.

"No, I haven't seen them," she said. "I hope they don't cause any more trouble."

"Where's Star?" I asked, changing the subject quickly.

"She's with Mara and Bessie. They've gone to pick berries and sea grapes down the path."

I ran down the trail that led into the woods and out to the shore. After a short distance I could hear voices.

"Star!" I called. "Supper's ready." I came to a wider section of the footpath. The sun shone through the branches of the trees, making flickering patterns in the clearing. I could see Mara and Bessie several feet away, moving among the low branches of the sea-grape trees.

Star was alone and sitting on the ground straight ahead of me, her long hair falling in her face. She had removed her sandal and was shaking out the stones. Then I saw another shadow on the path. Whatever it was moved along a branch above me.

I looked up and froze. High over Star's head, crouching in the twisted branches, was the panther, its golden eyes focused on my little sister!

S tar! Don't move," I called softly, not wanting to startle her or the panther. I was sure the panther hadn't seen me, as I was still on the path in the thicket. Star's eyes lit up when she saw me, and she was about to speak. "Shh! Be quiet," I said.

Star looked puzzled, but she did as I said. However, before I could reach her, the panther leaped from the canopy of leaves overhead, landing about five feet from my sister. I surged forward, clapping my hands and yelling as loudly as I could. "Get outta here! Scram! Yaaahhh!"

The huge cat was startled, and it turned toward me with a snarl. I'd never been so scared. My skin felt icy, and I thought I would throw up. Suddenly the panther veered directly toward Mara and Bessie.

I scooped Star up into my arms and screamed, "Mara! Panther! Run!"

Mara's piercing shriek cut through the under-brush. "Jake, help us!" I could hear Bessie howling.

I raced with Star toward the clearing. Bessie and Mara, frozen in fear, clung to each other as the panther crept toward them, its ears back and its tail straight out. I looked for a rock or stick that I could throw at the animal, but I couldn't find any-thing.

"Help us!" Mara screamed again and again.

Suddenly, from the waterfront, two silhouettes appeared. Rudy and Jewel! Rudy, growling and barking, raced toward the huge cat. I was afraid of what was about to happen, thinking of Ripper. One bite of those fangs and Rudy would be dead instantly!

Then Jewel blasted out with that honking whinny of hers and galloped toward the ruckus at full speed. As if with years of coordinated practice, Rudy circled the panther, drawing it away from Mara and Bessie, and the confused cat backed away, right into Jewel's path. Jewel reared up on her hind legs, then came crashing down, her front hooves aimed directly at the panther's midsection. The panther rolled over, howling, then picked itself up and tried to dart by Rudy into the brush. But Rudy put himself between the cat and the undergrowth, barking all the while.

Jewel was following that panther like a shadow. This time she bent down and grabbed the cat by the nape of the neck, shook it like a scatter rug, and tossed it into the bushes. The injured animal tried to hobble away, but Jewel was still not satisfied. She bounded over to the panther for a final kick. Rudy waited nearby, then went to the wild cat and sniffed at it. The panther lay still.

"Is it dead?" Mara asked in a shaky voice.

"I think so." I went to Jewel and stroked her sweaty neck. "What a gem you are, Jewel." She shook her head and nickered. Rudy trotted to me and hit my leg with his paw as if to say, *Are you all right, Jake?*

I got down on my knees to hug him. "You're pretty precious yourself, Rudy. Good dog!"

Bessie and Star trotted over to Rudy and threw their arms around him. The dog wagged his whole body and licked their faces.

Sharkey broke through the brush and called as he ran toward us, "What happened? I heard noise and screams." He looked bewildered as we all spoke at once. "Are you telling me that Jewel and Rudy killed the panther?"

"Go see for yourself," I said, pointing to the animal. "The panther was going after Mara and Bessie. I don't know what would have happened if Jewel and Rudy hadn't shown up."

Sharkey nudged the panther with his boot. "It's dead all right. Cougars out west will attack people occasionally, if they're wounded or if food is scarce. But this is the first Florida panther I've ever seen stalk anyone."

"You and Rudy are heroes," I told Jewel.

"I've never been so frightened!" Mara's hands were trembling as she stroked Jewel's neck. "Thank you, Jewel, you wonderful mule. No one in this town will complain about either of you ever again once I tell them how you saved us."

Jewel snorted with her whinny-bray, and Rudy wagged his tail in agreement.

Mara was right. For the next month after the panther episode, everyone in town treated Jewel and Rudy as the heroes they were and gave them the best of everything. Folks brought bags of hay and fruit for Jewel and slices of meat and leftovers for Rudy. No one yelled at Jewel if she chomped off a star fruit or two from their trees; nor could anyone resist Rudy when he came calling at dinnertime and begged with his outstretched paw. Since Ripper was gone, the Robinsons welcomed Rudy with a pat and a treat. Miss Edith handed him a big piece of kielbasa sausage as an offer of apology. From then on, whenever they meandered by Miss Edith's cottage, she greeted them with *"Dzien dobry,"* which Mara said was Polish for "good day."

The word of Jewel and Rudy's heroism reached the veterans' camps, and workers came by to see the famous animals. Yes, Jewel and Rudy were celebrities, and they were smart enough to make the most of it. The mule and dog were allowed to walk anywhere in town as free as a breeze!

Early one morning a couple of weeks after the panther incident, I took Mara fishing. Mara brought a picnic basket filled with egg-salad sandwiches, fruit-filled *kolacki* cookies that Miss Edith had made, and a thermos of lemonade. Her auburn hair was tied back in a long braid, and instead of a dress she wore a pair of tan pants and a green shirt. Even in boys' clothes she was neat and pretty. As for me, well, I felt sloppy in my old shorts and oil-stained shirt. But Mara didn't seem to notice.

We climbed into the little dinghy my dad kept on the town dock, and I rowed us out onto the calm water.

The morning fog surrounded us in ghostly curtains. "It's as if we're on another planet, or in a dream," Mara said.

Gradually the morning sun lifted the fog, and the water began to sparkle. Mara plunked a straw hat on her head and tied it under her chin.

"You could pass for a conch today," I said as I pulled my sun visor out of my pocket and slapped it over my eyes.

"Good!" she said. "Once I learn to fish properly, I'll be a real, one-hundred-percent Florida conch."

I rowed and she sat in the stern with her hand dipped into the water. When we reached a cove where I knew we might catch some snapper, I pulled in the oars and threw down the anchor.

"Here," I said, handing her one of the fishing poles I had brought. "It's all ready to fish, except for the bait." I opened the pail of shrimp and pushed it toward her. "A real conch will know how to bait the hook."

Mara made a face as I placed a wiggling shrimp in her open palm. I showed her how to put the hook in a soft part, and then she tossed the line into the water.

I put bait on my hook and dropped the line on the other side of the dinghy. Then I lay back across the seat and pulled the visor over my brow. "Now we just wait for a bite. Fish like the shade, and they'll get together under the boat," I told her in a whisper. "When you see that red and blue bobber start jumping, you'll know there's a nibble on the line."

"Is that all there is to it?" Mara asked.

"No, that's not all. When you get a bite, you'll have to pull that line just right to hook the fish."

We sat quietly for a while. Then Mara asked, "Who taught you to fish?"

"My dad."

"I thought it might have been Sharkey."

"Sharkey helped me with the bonefishing the other day," I said, "but it was my dad who taught me how to fish when I was a little kid. I never knew Sharkey well until recently."

"But now you're friends with him, right?"

Sharkey, a friend? I guessed that was true. We'd had a great time down in Key West. He taught me a lot about bonefishing, and he even showed me his secret fishing place. And every time I worked with him I learned something new, and had fun at the same time. "Yes, come to think of it, I'd say Sharkey really is my friend," I told Mara.

Suddenly her fishing pole began to twitch. "I've got a fish!" She jumped up, rocking the boat.

"Give him some line and then reel him in a little at a time." It looked like a snapper as it came closer to the surface. "Nice fish, Mara!" I said.

Mara was hopping up and down, and the boat was tipping even more.

"Don't jump around!" I warned, as I peered over the edge to see the fish more closely.

"Get the thing . . . the whatchamacallit!" Mara ordered.

I assumed she meant the net, so I grabbed it from the bottom of the boat. "I'll land him as you reel him in." Once again I leaned over, but this time water began to slip into the dinghy.

Mara leaned over too. "Jake! Get him!"

But now my weight plus Mara's on one side of the boat made the gunwales dip into the water. Before I could move to the other side and level the boat, I lost my balance and fell with a huge splash into the bay.

Mara's screams mixed with the gurgle of bubbles as I tumbled and kicked my way back up to the surface. "Oh, Jake! Are you all right?" she cried, leaning toward me, her hand outstretched. "I can't swim, or I'd come get you."

"I'm all right. Don't try to rescue me. Just get back to the middle of the boat!" She reached out again, and I called out in a stern voice, "Do not lean over like that!"

Mara looked sheepish and sat obediently on the middle seat.

But something was biting me—at least that's what it felt like. Something prickled against my rear and stung. A stingray? A jellyfish?

I kicked forward in a panic, only to have my legs tangle between both of our fishing rods, which had fallen overboard with me. One pole had a nice-size snapper attached to it. The other pole had *me* attached to it. I was hooked by the seat of my pants.

"I'm sorry, Jake. I've lost the fishing pole."

"No, you haven't," I replied. "It's right here." I unsnarled the lines and threw her pole into the boat—along with the flapping red snapper.

"Eeek!" Mara yelled. "It's flipping all over the place."

"Don't panic," I cautioned. "You'll tip the boat again."

She sat on the seat and pulled her feet up under her. "Get in, Jake. I don't know what to do with this fish."

I unhooked myself from my fishing rod and tossed it into the boat. Then I hoisted myself up. "Calm down and lean the other way," I told Mara. "You'll need to keep the boat stable as I climb on board."

Mara did as she was told and held the dinghy steady as I scrambled in.

"I'm so sorry, Jake." Mara was perched on the seat with her feet still pulled up. She pointed to the fish that was now flapping more slowly in the bottom of the boat. "Do something for that poor thing," she begged.

I pushed my dripping hair back from my eyes and realized I'd lost my visor overboard. *What a way to show Mara how to fish,* I thought miserably.

I reached for the slippery snapper, which wiggled out of my hands several times before I finally pulled the hook from its mouth.

"You'll have a nice fish dinner," I said as I dropped the fish into a pail.

"I . . . I don't think I could clean it, or . . . oh, Jake. I can't eat that fish. I'd feel awful. I mean . . ." Mara's brow wrinkled into a worried frown. "It's not the same as buying it in a store. I . . . I've come to know this fish in person, face to face. I've seen it alive. I couldn't eat it dead."

I was about to say I'd take it home to Mom, but I changed my mind. Mara would probably never forgive me for eating this snapper. "What do you want me to do with it?" I asked.

"Let it go, Jake. It should be set free."

I pulled it from the bucket and held it out over the edge of the boat. "Are you sure?"

Mara nodded, so I let the fish drop into the water. Mara and I watched as it lay there on the surface belly up for a moment, then popped over, wiggled its tail, and swam away.

After a few minutes we ate the sandwiches and *kolacki,* sipped lemonade, and watched pink spoonbills soar overhead.

Mara sighed. "This is nice. I love fishing."

I was soaking wet, had lost my visor, and had been hooked by my own line; the boat was ankle-deep in water, and we had no fish. I couldn't help but laugh out loud. "You love fishing?"

"Yes. I never dreamed it would be so much fun."

One morning in late August Sharkey said to me, "Folks will forget about Jewel and Rudy's bravery now the excitement is cooling, and they may consider them pests again. I need to get them under control."

So he and I finally hitched up the next two rungs on the fence. The gate worked well, and it still fastened with the cone-shaped wooden peg that fit tightly into place. "This should keep Jewel contained," he said. Sharkey paid me two more dollars for the work I did on the fence. Now that I had some money saved, I was thinking I might ask Mara to the movies up at Tavernier. The government sent films down for the veterans, and we locals were allowed to attend for a fee.

About a week later Dad and I were waiting for the train when Jewel and Rudy came meandering up the street, big as life. They had already made their usual stops at the hotel and the houses along the way.

"I thought you and Sharkey had the corral finished. How did Jewel get out?" Dad asked.

"Beats me. Sharkey keeps the gate latched, and now the fence is too high for Jewel to jump. At least I think it is. Of course, at this point nothing Jewel could do would surprise me."

Within ten minutes or so, Sharkey came down the road with a rope. He saw us at the train station and stopped. "Have you seen—"

"Yep, we saw them go by. Looks like they were heading toward the Robinsons' house," Dad answered.

"How did Jewel escape?" I asked, puzzled.

"You know that latch we made with the cone-shaped plug? Well, Jewel has figured out how to work it. I've noticed her investigating that latch as she hangs around the gate, and I saw her chewing on the plug a few times. Then today, by golly, she pulled it clear out of the lock with her teeth and pushed open the gate."

"I don't believe it!" Dad said, laughing.

"Believe it, Doug," Sharkey said. "That mule is just too intelligent for the likes of us ordinary humans!"

The following day Sharkey saddled up Jewel and took her for a ride. I stayed behind with Rudy and added a knotted rope to the gate. "Until Sharkey gets a lock and chain, Jewel will have to chew a lot more rope in order to escape," I told Rudy, who sat by watching me. "Maybe she'll get discouraged and stay put for a change." When Sharkey returned, he was grinning like an alligator.

"She's a good riding mule, that's for sure. Most mules run when they see you coming with a harness or saddle. But not Jewel. She's only too glad to oblige," he bragged. "And for your information, Jake, my feet don't drag on the ground. She's plenty big enough."

"You were right," I admitted.

He put Jewel back into the corral and we began painting Sharkey's boxcar—this time a bright shade of red paint that Dad had on sale. "This looks like a caboose," I said when we had finished one side of the car.

Just as we were getting ready to begin the other side, Mara and Star appeared from the road. "Hi, Jake!" Star called. She ran over and gave me a hug.

"We're real busy here, Star," I said, brushing her aside. Then she noticed Jewel all saddled up in the corral. "Can I have a ride on Jewel?" she asked Sharkey.

"Star, don't go around asking for things all the time," I said. "You're being a pest."

"I'm not a pest, Jake." Her mouth quivered and her eyes filled with tears.

Mara took Star's hand. "I'm sorry we bothered you, Jake. But we came to see Sharkey."

"You can have a ride, Star," Sharkey called, letting Jewel out of the corral. "Come on over here. Jewel's waiting for you." Star smiled and ran to him.

Sharkey lifted my sister into the saddle, and she beamed, although she was still wiping a few tears from her cheeks.

"It doesn't take much to be nice, Jake. Sharkey, Jewel, and Rudy are nicer to your sister than you are," Mara said, glaring at me. "Someday you'll regret all the mean things you say to Star."

"I'm sorry," I said meekly.

"Don't tell *me* you're sorry. Tell your sister."

Sharkey led Jewel around the house and down to the shore, with Rudy pacing along in front of them. Jewel walked slowly and gently, as if she knew to be careful with Star. I could hear Sharkey talking to Star. "Deep in the sand under there, baby turtles are waiting to hatch. Pretty soon they'll be digging their way out and heading to sea."

When the ride was over, I was the one who lifted Star off Jewel. "Did you have a nice ride?"

Star nodded but eyed me cautiously.

"Thank you, Sharkey," Mara said, ignoring me. "The reason we came by was to tell you that there's news about a hurricane heading this way. The veterans were talking about it at the post office this morning."

"I had heard something about a hurricane too," Sharkey said. "August is a bad time for storms, all right. But I also heard it's not likely to hit here."

"Let's hope not. We just thought we'd tell you, in case you needed to get prepared." Mara took Star's hand and headed up the path.

"Bye-bye, Rudy. Bye, Jewel. Bye, Jake." Star blew kisses to Sharkey. "Thank you for the ride, Sharkey!"

"Hey, Mara!" I called, trying to make amends. "Would you like to go fishing again this afternoon?"

Mara kept on walking and didn't answer.

Mom's Genuine American Oriental Rug

The next morning Star was sick with a fever. She was drowsy and hardly said a word.

"What's wrong with Star?" I asked.

"I don't know. I was up all night with her." Mom sat on the bed and placed a wet towel on Star's forehead. "Where do you hurt, honey?"

"My head aches," Star answered. Her eyes were puffy and glassy.

Mom motioned for me to follow her out of the room. "I'm going to need you to help today, Jake." Mom looked tired, with dark shadows under her eyes. "We've got to get Star's fever down."

"What can I do?"

"Bring up the pitcher of cold tea in the fridge downstairs. Tea is good for most everything. While you're down there, set up the sign at the counter."

Downstairs I put up the sign we used when

Mom couldn't serve breakfast or lunch. SORRY, THE LUNCH COUNTER IS CLOSED TODAY. Then I took the pitcher of ice tea to the upstairs kitchen and poured a glass for Star.

"Does Mara know that Star's sick?" I called to Mom.

"No. After you bring in the tea, please run over and tell Mara about Star," Mom answered from Star's room.

"Okay," I said eagerly. I wanted to see Mara and make things right with her. She'd been so mad at me the day before, I was afraid I'd lost her friendship.

As I hurried toward Star's room, I tripped on Mom's rug. Crash! Down I fell. The glass flew out of my hands and shattered as it hit the floor. The tea spread into a large dark spot on Mom's genuine American Oriental rug.

Mom came rushing out of the bedroom and looked at the mess in horror. "Oh, no! Not my rug! How could this happen!" She pulled a towel from the cupboard and began sopping up the tea.

"Let me sweep it first," I said, "before you cut your hand."

But it was too late. Mom's hand was already bleeding. She sat on the floor and burst into tears.

"I'm so sorry, Mom." I ran to the kitchen and fumbled in the drawers. "I'll get a bandage."

"Don't bother!" Mom wailed. "It's ruined. The one special, beautiful thing I own from my home in Georgia . . . and it's ruined!" Mom just sat there and cried like a child, her hands over her face, the blood from her cuts dripping down her arm. I tried to put my arms around her.

"It was an accident, Mom! I'm sorry. I know how you love that rug!" I was in tears myself seeing my mother's distress. I had never seen Mom cry so hard over anything. "I'll clean it up, Mom. I'll do such a good job you won't even notice. I promise."

"Just leave me alone and let me cry."

I picked up the pieces of glass, then soaked up the tea in the towel. After that I washed the spot in water and wiped the rug again.

Mom dabbed at her nose with her apron. "See? The stain is still there."

"That's because it's wet. When it dries, it won't show."

Star came out of her room. "What's wrong, Mommy? Why are you crying?"

"It's my rug. It's ruined."

"Can't you see how sorry I am?" I yelled as I ran down the stairs and out the door.

I was startled to see Mara coming up onto the porch. "I came for Star," she said.

I pushed by her. "Star's sick in bed."

"Where are you going in such a hurry?"

"I don't know—to the beach." I ran toward the path to the ocean, not wanting Mara to see that I had been crying.

Mom would never forgive me. That rug stood for all the things she left behind when she married Dad and moved to the Keys from Georgia: her family and friends, a house with indoor plumbing and electricity. I had ruined the one thing that reminded her of her old home. I couldn't stop the tears that now streamed down my face.

I ran all the way down to the waterfront and sat on the trunk of a palm tree that had been bent in a hurricane years ago. The ocean was calm and a greenish gray. The clouds overhead hung low, and

I wondered briefly about the hurricane that was out there somewhere.

I gazed along the shore and saw someone walking toward me on the beach. It was Mara. I reached down and threw seawater on my face, hoping she wouldn't be able to tell I'd been crying.

"Hi, Jake," she said as she came closer. "Are you okay?"

"No." I told her about the accident with the rug. "Mom will never forgive me. She cried and said I ruined the one special thing she owns. I feel awful."

"She'll forgive you." Mara sat next to me on the tree trunk, and we were both quiet for a long time.

Then I said, "It was my fault. I was clumsy and stupid. I'll never forget how she cried."

"Let it all blow away, Jake. That's what I have to do when I think of my father . . . and my mother. I've learned to let those sad feelings float up and disappear. Otherwise angry words and hurt feelings become storm clouds that follow you everywhere."

"You're not mad at me anymore? For the way I

spoke to Star?" I asked. "I was afraid I'd lost my best friend." I felt my face flush.

"I thought Sharkey was your best friend," Mara looked at me sideways with a teasing smile.

"Is there a law that says you can only have one best friend?" I asked.

"I guess not," Mara said.

"Besides, good things come in pairs," I said. "I'm sorry I said mean things to Star yesterday, but I'm not always that way, Mara. I do nice things for her too." I could feel my eyes filling up again. "I play with her, and I taught her how to swim, and I read to her, and I take her for walks . . ."

"Lullaby memories."

"What? I have no idea what you're talking about, Mara."

She laughed. "Lullaby memories are my happiest memories. When I'm sad I let them come out of my head and they soothe me—like lullabies."

"I hear you whistling a certain tune sometimes. Is it a lullaby?"

Mara laughed. "I didn't realize I did that until Aunt Edith said, 'A whistling woman and a crowing hen always come to some bad end.' I only half remember the tune. But I do remember that some-one sang it to me when I was very young, and I recall a pretty, smiling face over my crib."

"Your mother?"

"Yes." Mara took off her shoes and put her feet in the water. Neither of us spoke for a while. I could hear the sound of the palm fronds clicking in the breeze.

"Did your mother die when you were little?"

"No. She just went away—when I was about Star's age. We don't know where or why, although Daddy said she hated the coal mines. One day she was gone, and there was just Daddy and me left." Mara splashed her feet. "Sometimes I wonder if she ever really existed or if she was just a dream. But I do have those lullaby memories. I remember her rocking me. I remember her kissing me. I remember her face over my crib. So I know I had a mother once. She's not just a dream." She looked at me uncertainly. "I wrote a poem about saying good-bye to her. I let some of my feelings out, and it made me feel better to write it."

"I'd like to hear it," I said, and then added, "I might not understand it, though."

"It doesn't matter, Jake." She frowned a little. "I think I know it by heart."

She began to recite:

I've said good-bye and closed the door.
I've shut out the morning.
I've emptied the colors into little pools of tears
And let them be gone.
I've let winter come, I've let the flowers die,
And though sunbeams of memory
become smaller with time,
I hear the lullaby still.

I couldn't speak, because there was nothing to say. Mara had no one, except for her old aunt, Edith—and her lullaby memories.

"I will write a poem about Daddy some day," Mara said after a while. "I know I'll feel better when I do, but right now it's too hard for me. His death is so fresh in my memory, and it hurts too much."

"I want Star to remember the good things—not the mean words I've said to her."

Mara took my hand. "She will."

I squeezed Mara's hand and got up. "I'd better go home now. I'm hoping the storm with Mom is over."

After I said good-bye to Mara, I headed home to Mom and her genuine American Oriental rug. At least I knew that even if Mom was still angry, she'd be there waiting for me, as she always was. Mara would probably give anything to have a family like mine. Now I understood why she cared so much for Star, and why she tried to set me straight about Star and Mom.

I tiptoed up the stairs when I got home so I wouldn't wake Star if she was sleeping. I didn't want to make Mom mad about anything else. Mom was sitting at the kitchen table. She looked up when she saw me, and I saw that her eyes were swollen from crying, She motioned for me to come to her and I did.

Mom put her arms around me. "I'm sorry I was so hysterical, Jake. I'm overtired from not sleeping, and I've treasured that rug . . ."

"Mom, I would never intentionally hurt it in a million years."

"I know that." She gave me a kiss on the cheek.

"I'll get over it, Jake. Besides," she said more cheerfully, "you did a good job cleaning it up. The stain may not show that much."

"How is Star?" I asked.

"She's been sleeping off and on. She asked for you."

"I'll go in and see her."

Star was lying on her bed with just the sheet over her. I could feel the heat from her body when I entered the small room. "Hi, Jake," she whispered.

"Hi, twinkle star," I said. I dipped the towel in the pan of water Mom had left near the bed and patted her face and arms with it. Then I began to sing "Twinkle, Twinkle, Little Star."

"Sing it the nice way," Star mumbled.

As I held her hand and sang her song the nice way, Star closed her eyes and fell asleep.

Usually as Labor Day approached everyone in town prepared for a big barbecue picnic with local families. But this year, with Labor Day weekend only a few days away, the picnic was forgotten. Folks were preparing instead for the hurricane, in case it should veer our way. At the moment ships were reporting it would head toward Key West or even farther south, but everyone who lived on the Keys knew hurricanes only too well, and we understood how unpredictable and dangerous they could be. The only hurricane I remembered in my lifetime was when I was seven, and the eye of the storm missed us and went up to Lake Okeechobee. Still, I'd heard the stories of hurricanes past from the conchs who lived through them, and I grew to respect the howling wind and wild seas that had been known to bring ships onto the reefs.

To live on the Keys one had to acknowledge the power of storms.

With the possibility of a hurricane looming, Dad and I checked the barometer regularly, pulled hurricane shutters over the windows, and carried our outside display of fishing poles and paddles into the storeroom.

In the workers' camps, the Bonus Marcher veterans were uncertain whether they should take the train and leave the Keys or stay and face the storm. They waited for the government to give them orders, but so far none had come. "A hurricane couldn't be too bad," they reasoned, "or Uncle Sam would have ordered us from our shanties and taken us to the mainland for safety." I heard them talking at the store lunch counter about "how scared the locals are of a little wind."

"If there was a hurricane coming, the government would warn us," Milt Barclay told Dad. "But no one seems to be worried."

"That's right," Harry Webber agreed. "They'll get us off the Keys if there's danger."

"It'll be too late if the storm catches you inside those little huts and tents," Dad told them.

"I've never been in a hurricane," another vet said. "But hey, we need a little excitement around here."

Dad and Mom looked at each other with raised eyebrows. "Trust me, you don't want that kind of excitement," Mom said. "You have no idea—"

Harry interrupted her. "We survived the war and the trenches in France. Surely we can survive a little windstorm!"

"Besides, the weather forecasters predict that it will hit Havana, Cuba. Why waste time getting ready for a storm that will never come?" Milt scoffed.

Other veterans who were gathered at our lunch counter started chatting. Some of them were excited about the storm and seemed to actually hope the storm would strike our island.

Dad ignored them and continued with our preparations. We had extra kerosene lanterns cleaned and filled, and we put candles at the counter and on the tables because it was dark in the store with the windows covered. Dad filled up gas cans for the generator.

Star was still feverish, and Mom tried calling

Dr. Whiteside, the nearest doctor, but there was no answer. "Maybe he's gone up to the mainland," Mom said worriedly.

Later that day Rudy showed up, scratching and barking at the store door. "What do you want, boy?" I asked. Rudy ran out into the road, circled, and came back, barking.

"What's wrong?" I asked. Rudy circled again, and this time when he came back he took hold of my shirt in his teeth. *Something is wrong.*

Rudy raced down the road, then stopped and barked, as if to say, *Come on! Hurry up, Jake!*

I followed the dog up the road and then down the path to Sharkey's place. "Sharkey?" I yelled when I came close to his house. "Sharkey!"

Suddenly I saw him lying on the ground near the corral. Jewel stood solemnly nearby like a sentry keeping watch. She put her head down to Sharkey and nudged him with her nose. I ran to him. "Sharkey!"

"It's my leg. It gave out on me and . . ." He tried to pull himself up, but he couldn't. "Blasted Jerry who caught me with his bullet." He grimaced in pain and cursed several times.

I helped him to a sitting position, with his back against the fence post for support. "Why are you so mad?"

"Because it hurts!"

"Maybe you need a doctor. Mom tried to reach Dr. Whiteside for Star, but there's no answer."

"I'll be all right now that I'm up. I just need to sit here for a while." He reached out and patted Rudy, who had hunkered down next to him.

"Rudy brought me here," I told him.

"Good boy," he whispered to Rudy, whose tail thumped a few times. "How did I manage without you and Jewel?"

"Can I get you anything, Sharkey?"

"I've got crutches hanging on the wall inside the hut."

"I'll get them." I ran to the boxcar and pulled up the screening that Sharkey had rigged to hang over the open doors. This was the first time I'd ever been inside Sharkey's place, and I expected it to be a sloppy mess. However, the place was in perfect order. One section was set aside for a kitchen area, with a small kerosene stove and a sink that connected to the cistern outside. A fork, spoon, and knife were set on the table ready for the next meal. A feeling of sadness swept over me for some reason I couldn't explain.

"Jake!" Sharkey yelled from outside. "What are you doing in there? The crutches are right by the door."

I turned around, and there were the crutches, just as he said. I grabbed them off the hook and carried them out to Sharkey, who was struggling to stand up. He placed them under his armpits and sighed. "Guess I'll be using these for a while."

"Take it easy for a few days, Sharkey," I said.

Sharkey headed painfully to his boxcar with Rudy at his heels. "I can't take it easy. There's a storm coming. I was trying to batten down the hatches when I twisted my leg."

I followed him in and helped him get settled on the couch. We propped up his swollen leg with a cushion, and then I gave him some pills that he pointed out on the sink.

"Last time I saw Doc he gave me these to use if I have a lot of pain. I try not to use them except in an emergency."

"I'd say this is an emergency, Sharkey," I said, handing him a glass of water.

"And then there's the hurricane. I thought it might miss us, but the air is heavy, and, well, now I'm thinking we will get the storm full force."

"Dad and I will help you close up." I peered out the door toward the bay. It was calm, reflecting the trees along the shore. Big puffy clouds sailed serenely across the sky. No sign of a storm. "Don't worry, Sharkey. It's supposed to go below the Keys—near Cuba, anyway. It'll probably miss us."

"I don't think so, Jake. Like I said, I have a bad feeling about this storm."

Dad and I took turns staying with Sharkey for the next two days, but it was impossible to keep him off his feet for any length of time. No matter what he asked me to do to get his property ready for the storm, he'd interfere. Then he'd get up with his crutches and come over to inspect my work.

"I'll do it, Sharkey. That's why I'm here!" I'd yell.

"Then do it right!" he'd yell back.

Eventually, once we had everything secured outside, I attached Sharkey's motorboat to his old boat trailer, and then I hooked Jewel up to the front of the trailer. After a few prompts Jewel pulled the boat out of the water and onto the shore. Of course, Rudy sat in the trailer as if cheering Jewel on.

"Now you know why it's good to own a mule!" Sharkey said. "Especially with a hurricane coming."

"Do you really think we'll get the storm?"

"Of course I do. Didn't you hear me say I have a bad feeling about this hurricane? We've got to be prepared. You ought to know that, Jake."

Once we hung up all the tools in the shed and got them out of the way, I was able to push the trailer inside. "We'll keep the wagon out for now, in case we need it," Sharkey ordered. So I got Jewel to pull the wagon near the entrance to his house.

"What about Jewel and Rudy? How are you going to keep them contained?" I asked.

"Haven't you noticed they've been staying home lately? I have a chain with a lock that I put on the corral when I want to keep Jewel in one place. Unless Jewel has become a locksmith recently, I don't think she can open the gate anymore."

On Sunday of the Labor Day holiday weekend, I hitched Jewel up to the wagon to bring Sharkey over to our house for breakfast.

"I didn't hear the church bells this morning," Sharkey said as we rattled along the dirt road.

"Folks won't be going to services today," I said, "not when a big storm is brewing."

"God helps him who helps himself," Sharkey muttered, looking out at the bay. "No sense sitting around waiting for a miracle. Not when those clouds are whisking up from the south and the sea has that dark, threatening look."

"The vets who come to our store say the storm isn't coming," I told Sharkey. "If it were, the government would send a train to get them out."

Sharkey shook his head. "One would hope so, but I don't believe anything until I see it. Back in 1906, when I was a young buck working on the overseas railroad, a group of our construction workers were out on Long Key when a storm was brewing. Supervisors paid no attention and refused evacuation. The hurricane came, and the men on Long Key were killed."

"Lucky you weren't with them."

"Lucky indeed," Sharkey said.

When we arrived at the store, Dad had his sleeves rolled up and was checking the engine in the truck. "I've tried everything to get this engine going. It goes for a while, but then it dies."

"You can only nurse it along for so long, Doug," Sharkey said. "It's been on its last legs for months now."

"If I could get it going, we could take Star to a hospital." Dad slammed the hood down. "We've got to get help for her."

"Is there anyone else who could take her?"

"Most everyone with a car or truck has gone," Dad said.

"Even if you got the truck going, with this engine you might get stuck in the middle of nowhere," Sharkey warned. "And the storm surge on this flat land could come right up and over the Keys. You could be swept away."

"Maybe we could get a ferry down to Key West," I suggested.

"The ferry isn't running," Dad said. "The seas are too rough."

Dad and I helped Sharkey out of the wagon, then tied Jewel to the old gumbo-limbo tree. Rudy sat on the porch.

"Mom's busy upstairs. Star is still feverish, and your mother is constantly cooling her down, giving her water to drink—and doing a lot of praying," Dad went on. "Mara's here to give Mom a hand."

"What about Miss Edith?" I asked. "We should check out her house too."

"Billy and Roy went with their dad to close up the shutters. That house should be okay. It's been through dozens of storms," Dad said.

In the downstairs kitchen Mara had cooked bacon and eggs at the lunch counter. "It's hard to believe all this talk about a storm coming," she said. "There's hardly a breeze."

"The calm before the storm," Sharkey said.

We sat at a table and Mara served breakfast.

"Star just fell asleep again," Mom said as she came down the stairs and sank into a chair. She looked exhausted and worried, and her eyes were rimmed with dark circles. "Did you get the truck running?" she asked Dad.

"It starts up, then stops," Dad answered.

"Doug, the veterans have a clinic up near Snake Creek. I don't know why I didn't think of it before," Mom said. "If you can get the truck working, we could take Star up there to a doctor."

"It's only for the veterans," Dad told her. "One

of the fishermen became ill and went to that place, and they wouldn't touch him. Something about government policy and insurance. I doubt if they'd take care of Star."

"But this is an emergency!" Mom insisted. "It's going on four days now that she's been running this fever. We can't just sit here and do nothing."

"I don't dare take the chance of getting stuck in the storm," Dad said.

Mara passed Mom a plate with a muffin and guava jelly, then poured her a cup of coffee. "Thank you, dear. You're becoming another daughter to me." Mom smiled weakly at Mara but pushed the food away. "I wish I could reach Dr. Whiteside. Star complains of a bad headache, and her fever goes so high."

"He's probably gone to the mainland," Sharkey said. "Just about everyone else has left—either because they had plans for the holiday or now because of the hurricane."

"Let's check the forecast." Dad turned on the radio and fiddled with the dial.

"The warm waters off the Florida peninsula are strengthening the storm, which is now a full-fledged

hurricane. The direction is westward at about eight miles per hour. The hurricane is expected to move across the Straits of Florida and into the Gulf of Mexico late tonight or early Monday. Hurricane pennants are now displayed from Fort Pierce to Fort Myers on the west coast. Look for gales and high tides on the Florida Keys."

"It doesn't sound as if it's coming here," Mom said hopefully.

Dad shook his head. "Lou, fishermen who've been out at sea and have made it back are telling about big swells blowing in from the southeast. If the waves keep coming from that direction, I'm afraid we'll get the storm."

"I took a walk to the beach this morning," Mara said. "I didn't see any breakers, but a lot of seaweed had drifted onto the beach."

"We don't usually see breakers. The coral reefs break up the waves before they come into shore," Dad explained.

"There was a nice sunset last night over at Sharkey's," I said, trying to be optimistic. "You know what they say: 'Red sky at night, sailors delight.'"

"Cirrus clouds make colorful sunsets," Sharkey said, "but they're still signs of an approaching storm."

"I'm more inclined to believe the scientists at the weather bureau than to listen to those silly old superstitions," Mom sniffed.

"Lou, honey," Dad said, "you don't want to believe the hurricane is coming here, and neither do I. But the fact is that despite what the weather bureau is saying, we know from the signs that it will strike very close to Islamorada, and we have to be prepared."

"I know," Mom said, her eyes filling with tears. "My hope is that the forecasters are right. I just can't face a hurricane—not with Star so ill." She started up the stairs, then paused. "Keep trying to get the truck working, Doug. Maybe we can get to the clinic at Snake Creek in the morning." She turned to me. "And Jake, please stay with us tonight. I'm sure Sharkey will understand that I want our family to be together right now."

"Yes, he should be here with you," Sharkey agreed. "Things will work out for all of us, Lou."

"Thank you, Sharkey," Mom said. "I hope so."

Later in the afternoon Sharkey was ready to go home, so I helped him into the wagon. "Where's Rudy?" he asked. "Well, let's go without him," Sharkey said. "Can't wait around all day."

Jewel looked anxiously toward the path that led to the shore. It was windy, and her black mane blew in the gusts. She snorted and did her whinny-bray. "She's looking for Rudy. Why don't we ride down and find him," I suggested. "Jewel behaves better when Rudy's around."

I didn't have to lead Jewel. She knew where to find Rudy and took us down the path that led to the church, and along the shore to the Ashburns' place. Sure enough, Rudy was sitting by the closed door, waiting patiently to see Ginger.

"Come on, boy," Sharkey yelled. "This is no time to be visiting your girlfriend."

Billy and Roy came out from around the side of the house. They were wearing carpenter aprons, and Roy had a hammer in his hand. "Hi, Jake! Do you need any help battening down?" he called.

"We're all set, thanks," I answered. "Is Miss Edith's place secure?"

"We put up her shutters," Billy answered. "She and Mara are all set."

Mr. Ashburn stuck his head out the door. "I've heard the storm's slowed down—another sign it will turn north," he called out to us. "Better take cover soon."

"Thanks. We're on our way," Sharkey answered.

"We're too close to the ocean here. If it gets real bad, I'm taking my family up to the packinghouse on the railroad bed," Mr. Ashburn yelled from the porch. "It's higher ground there."

"Good idea. A storm surge shouldn't come up that far." Sharkey looked out at the ocean. "The waves are breaking close to shore now, and they're from the south. Come on, Rudy. Get on board."

This time Rudy bounded down the stairs at Sharkey's command, and he leaped into the wagon, plopping down next to Sharkey. "Giddap, Jewel," I said. The mule shook her mane and plodded up the path.

When we got back to Sharkey's I asked, "Where should we put Jewel?"

"Over in that lean-to shed," he answered. "That

should hold her for now. Rudy can come into the house with me."

"Then I'd better tie Jewel up. You shouldn't come out in the storm, Sharkey. No matter what. Not with your bad leg."

"I'll be okay," Sharkey said. "We're on the lee-ward side, and the wind won't be so bad over here."

After I left Sharkey, I went home. Star was crying with her headache. Mom gave her some kind of herbal medicine she had on hand, and she fell back to sleep again. "She's burning up," Mom said, removing Star's sweaty pajamas and putting on another pair. "Poor baby." She kissed Star's hot tummy while Mara looked on anxiously.

It was muggy and hot upstairs in the house, so Dad opened one window shutter, and we sat in the living room with the radio on low.

"Want to play rummy?" I asked. "It'll pass the time."

Mom poured limeade and we played, but it wasn't much fun. We were too worried about Star and the storm.

Suddenly we looked up in surprise. Star had come out from her room and was walking toward us. Mom got up and went to her. "Star, where are you going?"

"To the baby turtles," Star answered.

"Baby turtles?" Mara said. "Where?"

"I want to see the baby turtles."

"Not now, honey," Mom said. But Star kept walking toward the stairs that led down to the store. "Careful, Star," Mom said, grabbing her hand. "You're too sick to go downstairs."

Star stood near the stairway in a daze. Her face was flushed with fever, and her hair clung around her face in sweaty curls.

Mara gasped. "She's walking in her sleep."

"She's delirious," Mom whispered. "Oh, why didn't we take her away from here yesterday? We've got to get her to a doctor." She led Star back to her room. Star stared straight ahead, not seeing anything. She walked with little steps and would have wandered off in other directions had not Mom held her hand firmly. Mom's face was pale, and I'd never seen her so frightened. Dad followed her to Star's room, and I could hear them talking quietly.

"Star is so sick, she doesn't know where she is

or what she's doing," Mara said softly. "I wish I could do something for her."

Mom reappeared with tears trickling down her cheeks. "You can do something, Mara. She loves you, and you're so good with her. Perhaps you can talk to her, or tell her a story—anything to keep her content. I'm so afraid that she . . ." Mom covered her face with her hands and turned away.

Mara went with Mom to Star's room, while Dad came and sat with me at the table.

"Mom doesn't want you to worry, but she's afraid that Star might have sleeping sickness," Dad said, and his voice broke. "She has all the symptoms—high fever, delirium, headache."

"No, not Star!" I cried out. Everyone had heard of the sleeping sickness. One of my classmates had had it the year before and was taken to the mainland. I never heard what happened to her.

"Mom is going to keep her cool all night and give her sweet catnip tea and feverfew for her headache. It's only herbal treatment, but it's about all we can do for now." Dad patted my shoulder. "With a hurricane on the way, the regular train service will stop. However there may be a train for the veterans tomorrow, and if so, perhaps we can get Mom and Star on board."

"But, Dad," I protested, "you heard Milt and Harry say the government hadn't sent any orders to get them off the Keys!"

"Maybe help will come tomorrow."

I circled my arms on the table and buried my face in them. *Please help us, God,* I prayed silently. *Save my little sister.* I felt a tight knot in my gut. *Please save Star.*

The wind was rising outside, and above the sounds I could hear Mara singing.

Sweet little sleepyhead, close your eyes
And hear the soft wind blowing.
While way up in the starry skies
A summer moon is glowing.
Sweet little sleepyhead, close your eyes
To dream of a bright tomorrow,
With blue balloons and merry tunes
And never a tear or sorrow.

A gust of wind rattled through the window that Dad had left open. He got up and closed it, then looked at the barometer on the wall. "It's dropping," he whispered to me. "That storm is heading for us. If the veterans' train doesn't come tomorrow, we'd better face the fact that we'll be trapped right here in Islamorada."

Later, in the early evening, Mom took a nap while Star slept. Mara and I sat together in Star's room to keep an eye on her. Mara kept patting Star down with wet cloths. Whenever Star roused, Mara got her to sip a little watered-down tea.

"Good girl," Mara whispered, and kissed Star's head. "You'll get better soon, sweetie."

"Mara, maybe you should stay here with us during the storm."

"No, I need to be with Aunt Edith. I'm sure we'll be fine. She told me she's gone through some powerful storms before. The house is anchored to the ground, and the Ashburns helped put up the hurricane shutters. It's gloomy inside, but other than that we should be safe."

Dad came to Star's door overhearing our conversation. "It's not just the winds," he said. "There could be a storm surge and that means flooding. So be aware of the rising water, Mara."

"What should we do if the water rises?" Mara asked.

"Get to high ground as soon as you see it's getting higher," Dad told her. "I'm sure Miss Edith knows the dangers."

It was getting dark when Mom woke up. "Thank you, Mara dear," she said. "I feel better having taken a nap. You've been a tremendous help." She turned to me. "Walk Mara home, Jake. She shouldn't go back alone."

Mara hugged my mother and father. "My prayers are with Star—and with all of you."

"Stay safe, Mara," Mom and Dad said together.

I took a flashlight and was glad I did, because the sky was black and without a star. As we walked along the railroad bed toward Miss Edith's house, not a light could be seen through the trees, since most everyone's windows were shuttered tight. Occasionally a gust of wind rattled the palms, but other than that there was an eerie stillness that permeated our little town.

Mara reached out and took my hand. "Jake, I'm scared."

I squeezed her hand hard. "It will be over in no time. The storm comes, and then it's gone, just like any other storm. Things will go back to normal. You'll see."

"You know, Jake, I love it here in the Keys. I feel as though I belong here now." She laughed. "I wish I could stay here forever."

"Why can't you stay here forever? You're a real conch now. And a fisherman, too."

"That one lesson doesn't make me a fisherman!" Mara said.

"Well, you may need another lesson," I agreed. "Conchs are great fishermen."

We both laughed. Mara slapped at a mosquito. "This is the first time since Daddy died that I've felt part of a family—even though it's *your* family."

"We all think of you as one of us," I told her.

"I'm glad you do. Back where I lived, most coal miners have large families—especially Polish families like ours. Some have nine or ten children. But my family was just Daddy and me. After Daddy's accident I wondered if I'd ever belong anywhere or be happy again."

"Tell me about your dad."

"Daddy was tall and handsome and a very kind man. He worked long hours in the mines, so we didn't have much time together. But the little time we had was special, full of love and fun. We'd take walks together, and he'd sing with me. We were real close. Like your family."

We walked silently for a while, and then Mara stopped. "Jake, I have a scary feeling that something is about to happen."

"Well, of course you do, with all the talk about the storm."

"It's not the storm that scares me."

"What is it, then?"

"It's hard to explain. Remember when I told you about the culm banks after a snowstorm? When I was coasting over them in the cold, fresh air, I forgot the blackness underneath."

"But that was good, wasn't it?"

"It was wonderful. Staying here is like that. I feel happy and free and . . . it's as if I've been given a gift, a space in time to be in this beautiful place with the flowers and the sea, and especially to be with your family, with little Star, with Aunt Edith, and Sharkey . . ."

"And Jewel and Rudy," I added.

"Yes, even Jewel and Rudy." She chuckled and then became serious again. "I needed all of you."

"We need you, too," I told her. "Mom said you're like another daughter to her. But being here isn't like sledding on the culm banks," I said. "This is real. The sunshine, the sea, the flowers . . . everything. There's no black coal underneath it all."

Mara went on. "For me it feels as if the snow is melting, and soon everything will be gone. It's too good to last, Jake."

"Why? You can stay here forever."

"There is no forever—not for me, or for anyone." She touched my arm. "Last night I stayed up really late and wrote a little verse about being here. Want to hear it?"

"Sure I do."

"Don't try to figure it out. Just listen." She cleared her throat. "I hope I can remember it all. I call it 'Borrowed Cottage.'"

Will I return to this place someday
To watch the sunset on the bay?
Will the sea be as green another year?
Night skies as still and deep and clear?

Mara watched my face. "Are you listening?"
"Yes, I am. There's more, right?"
Mara took a deep breath and went on.

Many waiting rainbows yet will span
The puffy clouds above the sand,
And where my gulls soar in the sky,
Other wings must beat and fly.
This place on earth we only borrow.
So soon the night, so soon tomorrow.

"Wow, Mara. That's really beautiful," I said. "It's kind of sad, though." I didn't understand why she should feel gloomy when she loved being here on the Keys. "You're still depressed about losing your dad, aren't you?"

"I've come to accept it, Jake. Life is like that borrowed cottage in my poem."

✳

We started walking again, hand in hand, not saying anything for a while. Then Mara whispered, "Thanks, Jake, for being such a good friend to me."

"I always will be your friend. We'll have lots of good times together yet," I said in a husky voice. "Neither of us will be blown away in the storm, you know."

"I sure hope not!"

"You write deep poems, Mara."

"It's a good way to get feelings out. You should try it sometime."

"Aw, I'm not eloquent like you are."

"Eloquent!" She giggled. "That's a great word, Jake. I'll bet you could write poetry if you tried."

I grinned. Usually words like "eloquent" didn't come easily to me. It made me feel good.

Down on the road a group of laughing veterans passed us in a pickup truck. "They don't seem a bit concerned about the storm," Mara said. "They're probably counting on the government to send a train for them."

"Dad said the train should come for them before the storm hits. Their huts are made of light wood, and some just have canvas roofs. They'll never stand up in high winds," I told her. I had to talk louder, as the wind was now gusting.

"Your dad said to be aware of rising water. Can the sea come in this far?"

"I suppose it could with a storm surge." I flashed the beam of my flashlight down over the embankment to the road. "See how much higher we are on this bed of train tracks than the ground on either side? Perhaps this mound would act as a dam, trapping the water."

"If it did, seawater on the east side could build up, couldn't it?" she asked. "We're on the east side."

"Yes, that's why Dad told you to watch out for rising water."

"If the government sends a train, perhaps they'd take us, too, and we could all get off the Keys."

"We'll know more in the morning. I sure wish we could get Star to a doctor," I said.

We had reached Miss Edith's house. The shutters were down, and everything looked dark.

"Thanks for walking me home, Jake." To my

surprise, Mara gave me a hug. "Good night, Jake. Stay safe."

"Stay safe," I said, hugging her back.

We both laughed nervously, but as I headed home, I thought about the things she'd said to me—her feeling that things had been too good to last, and the part of her poem that went: *This place on earth we only borrow. So soon the night, so soon tomorrow.*

I would remember those words forever.

None of us slept well Sunday night. Star was up walking around a couple of times in her delirium, and Mom had spells of crying. Dad kept watch over the barometer regularly. Then he'd make the announcement that it was "dropping fast," which would make me get up and look for myself. Sure enough the needle had dropped to 28.6 inches, and it had been 29 a short while ago. People living in the Keys, especially fishermen, counted on barometers. We learned how to read them in school, so I knew that normal was around 30 or 31. But neither Dad nor I had ever seen the needle drop like this. The pressure dropping this low meant a storm was coming for sure—and soon!

Outside, gusts of wind whistled around the

windows, and rain splattered on the roof now and then, but still it was nothing alarming.

When dawn came, we peeked out the front door. The sky was murky, and the clouds seemed to descend just above the trees. The breaking of waves on the beach was loud enough for us to hear from our porch.

"Come on, Dad. While Mom and Star are sleeping, let's take a walk to the shore and see what's going on for ourselves," I suggested.

"All right," Dad agreed. "It might be a good idea to take a look and get an indication of what we might expect."

Little spurts of rain splashed in our faces as we headed to the beach. At the church dock we saw large waves rising and falling over the reefs offshore, then rolling toward us to crash on the beach. The clear green waters had turned into frothing bubbles and seaweed. "It's coming directly at us," said Dad.

When we returned home, Star was whimpering and Mom was trying to get her to drink some juice. Dad checked the barometer again. "Now it's down to 27.8."

Milt Barclay and some other veterans stopped by in the old army truck to see if we were open for breakfast. "Not when there's a hurricane coming," Dad told them.

"We're all off today because of the holiday, not because of the storm," Harry Webber said. "You could make some money if you were open."

"Haven't you seen the clouds out there? They're black, and so low you can stick your head right through them," Dad retorted.

"We haven't been evacuated," Harry said.

"So we're enjoying the holiday, despite a few clouds. And we sure could use a cup of java," said Milt.

"No coffee today," Dad told them. "We're keeping an eye on our sick little girl as well as the storm. And you fellows should be preparing. Those huts you live in won't last five minutes in a gale, never mind a hurricane."

"The mess hall is a strong building. We can always go there to get away from the wind," Harry said. "But we're not worried. The government will send a train to get us if there's real danger."

"Let's go back down to camp since we can't get any coffee here," Harry said. "They'll have some ready in the mess hall by now."

"Say, Harry, do you suppose you could take Star and her mother to the veterans' clinic at Snake Creek?" Dad asked.

"Not possible," Harry said. "We can't take passengers in this truck—other than government people. Something to do with insurance."

"They're real strict about that rule. We could lose our jobs," Milt added. "Wish we could help you out, though, Doug."

"If you hear that the rescue train is coming, let us know, please. We've got to get Star out to the mainland to a doctor."

"Sure, if we know anything about a train, we'll get word to you."

The veterans took off in the army truck. I watched it rumble down the road and out of sight, not realizing then that this would be the last time we'd see Milt Barclay and Harry Webber.

By noontime the winds were blowing a gale, and Mr. Ashburn came by with Billy and Roy. They showed us a banner they had found that had washed up on the shore. STORM ADVISORY. GET TO PORT was the message.

"Several boats have come into port with these signs," Roy told us.

"They were dropped by the Coast Guard planes," Billy added excitedly.

"And now a hurricane flag has been hoisted at the lighthouse out there on Alligator Reef." Mr. Ashburn shook his head. "The ocean is already creeping onto some of the low-lying roads. This is going to be a bad one, Doug."

"Strange thing, though," Dad said. "The weather bureau still maintains that it's going south of us—down in the straits near Key West."

"Don't count on the weather bureau. They're dead wrong. You and I both know that the storm's on its way to Islamorada and we'll get the heft of it. None of us conches are taking any chances."

Roy nodded. "That's right. The hotel's all boarded up."

"God help those veterans out there in the

camps with their flimsy huts. I hear their buildings are already starting to fall apart in the winds," Mr. Ashburn said.

Later we ate lunch upstairs to be near Star, who was sleeping on the couch. I slapped together some bologna sandwiches for all of us.

Dad looked at the falling barometer. "It's down to 27.4 now," he said. "I don't remember ever seeing the barometer fall this low. The storm must be almost on us."

"Will Mara and Miss Edith be okay over there by themselves?" I asked.

"The wind has battered that house many a time," Mom said.

"And it's anchored onto rock-solid coral," Dad added.

"Maybe we should go check on Sharkey before it gets any worse. With his bad leg . . ."

"Sharkey can fend for himself," Dad said. "He's an old salt, and he's weathered lots of hurricanes."

"But what will he do with Jewel? The only shelter she has is that old lean-to," I said.

"Jake, Sharkey knows we have our own family to take care of," Mom said. "Don't worry about him or Jewel. Sharkey loves those animals, and he'll find a way to keep them safe. Once the storm passes, you and Dad can go over there and see if they're okay."

By late afternoon the wind raged against our wooden house as if giants were rattling the shutters.

"The wind wants to come in," Star mumbled.

"We won't let it in," I promised. But I could feel the gusts slyly creeping over the windowsills and around the door frames. Suddenly, *crack!* A shutter rattled, then blew off, smashing the kitchen window. The wind exploded into the room in a fury, tearing the curtains and shades and whipping the tablecloth onto the floor.

Star came out of her sleep and screamed. "Make the wind go away, Jake! Make it go away!"

I looked at Dad helplessly. "It will go away soon," I promised Star.

"Let's find something downstairs that we can use to cover the window, Jake." He started for the stairs.

Dad and I hurried down to the store. Rivulets of water were slithering under the door. "It's raining in here," I said.

"Never mind that now." Dad motioned me to the back room, where we removed supplies from a shelf, then took a crowbar and pried the shelf from the wall. "This should do," he said. "It's about the size of the window."

We headed toward the front of the store and looked down at our feet. "I think the water is higher already."

Dad reached down, put his hand into the water, and then tasted it. "This isn't rain, Jake. It's salt water! The sea is coming in!"

I opened the front door to look outside. "No, Jake!" Dad yelled, but before I realized my mistake the wind blew it out of my hand and almost off the hinges. It took all our strength for Dad and me to pull that door shut against the wind. Dad stared at me, his eyes wide and fearful. "Oh my God, Jake, the sea is right outside! The ocean is overtaking us. The storm surge is coming directly into Islamorada." He pushed me in front of him. "Get upstairs, quick."

I raced up the stairs to our apartment with Dad following, hoisting the heavy shelving over his shoulders.

Mom was waiting at the top of the stairs. "What's happening?" she asked, tracking Dad to the open window.

"Hold this while I hammer," Dad said to me, ignoring her question. I held the shelving while he hammered big nails right into the wall and the sill.

"Doug! You know something. Tell me this instant!" Mom demanded.

Dad turned to her. "The sea is coming in downstairs."

"But our house isn't on the ocean," she said. "How can the sea be coming up this far?"

"I don't know!" Dad yelled. "But believe me, Lou, it is!"

Mom was quiet for a moment, and then she said urgently, "The hurricane is here inside our house. The wind is blowing the windows out; the ocean is creeping into the store. The whole house is shaking. We've got to get out of here."

"What are you saying?" Dad exclaimed.

"Let's get out while we can—before the house

caves in on us. We can drive the truck to the clinic. There will be a doctor there, and other people. We won't be alone. We could make it, Doug. I know we could make it."

"The clinic is way up on Windley Key and it's only for the veterans," Dad reminded her

"This is an emergency! They wouldn't turn us away," Mom pleaded, grabbing Dad's arm. "Please, Doug. How can it be any worse out on the road?"

"What if we get stuck? We'd be miles up the road with nowhere to go and a storm on top of us." Although Dad was arguing, I knew he was weakening. Another gust of wind struck the tree outside the broken window, and we could hear the branches shatter.

Mom swung around and grabbed a quilt from the couch. "If we wait any longer, we'll miss our chance." She put out her hand. In her palm were the keys to the truck.

"Mom, branches are flying off trees," I pleaded, "and the road could be underwater anywhere along the way."

"I can't stay here and watch us all perish." Tears poured from Mom's eyes. Her voice rose into a cry, and she stretched out her hand again. "Help us, Doug!"

"What about the rising water, Dad? Can we drive through it?" I asked.

"From what I can see, the water isn't as deep on the leeward side of the house where I parked the truck. It isn't even up to the hubcaps yet. We can get through the water if we go now. It's the engine I'm worried about."

Dad and Mom stared at each other for a long minute; then Dad took the keys. "Put your oilskins on, Jake. You'll have to sit in the back." He went to the closet and tossed me my yellow raincoat and hat, then pulled on his own as well. "Get Star ready, but wait inside until I get the truck started," he ordered Mom.

Dad and I went downstairs, where the water was now up to our ankles. When I opened the door, a gust pulled me bodily out into the yard. Through the shrieking of the storm I could hear the gushing of the crashing breakers. Other sounds mingled together—the rattling of palm fronds and shutters, the rain, the smashing of objects that were being hurled through the air.

"This is crazy," Dad muttered as we sloshed through the mud and debris.

I yanked off the canvas that covered the hood of the truck while Dad got behind the wheel and pulled the choke lever over and over. "I don't want to flood it," he yelled above the wind. "But it needs more gas because the engine's cold."

I held my breath as he turned the key and pushed the ignition. The engine coughed a few times, then died. Dad tried it again, and this time the motor sputtered, but as Dad adjusted the choke, it turned over and stayed. "Go get Mom and Star," he called to me.

Mom was already standing in the doorway with Star bundled in her arms. "Take her for me, Jake, while I get in." I took Star and held her close in the quilt to keep the rain off her face. I could feel the heat from her body as she slept through it all. Her periods of deep sleep made me even more fearful that she might have the sleeping sickness, as Mom had guessed.

Mom sloshed over to the truck, where Dad had already reached over and opened the door. Once she was inside, I placed Star gently in her lap.

"Get in the back, Jake. Quick!" Dad ordered.

I grabbed the canvas tarp and climbed in. It was dripping with rainwater, but it would protect me from the downpour to some degree. Dad backed up and was about to turn onto the road when—*crash!* A huge limb broke off from the gumbo-limbo tree and fell in our path. Dad paused, with the truck still running, while I jumped out and dragged the heavy branch far enough to the side of the road so Dad could drive around it.

"Get in!" Mom yelled. "Hurry!" I climbed back in and dove under the wet canvas. The branches of the bough scratched against me as Dad gunned the engine and steered around the fallen limb. I put my hands over my ears to drown out the screaming storm. Then I closed my eyes and prayed.

From under the tarp in the bed of the truck I could hear the storm's fury. Something landed with a crash and pounded me with a wallop. I peeked out and pushed a heavy board off me. Over the shouting winds I heard the muffled sound of Dad's voice. I peered into the back window of the cab and could make out his hands gesturing. He was wondering if I was all right, I figured, so I waved and hoped he could see me.

The early evening air was thick with hurtling objects and tiny, flickering lights that looked like fireflies. But as they hit sharply against my face, I realized they were hot grains of sand, and I held my hand to shield my eyes.

As we passed the train station, the lights from our truck revealed people struggling along the railroad bed toward the station or the packinghouse.

Was it the Ashburns, I wondered? Mr. Ashburn had said they planned to stay there for protection against any storm surge. The mound of earth that supported the railroad tracks and those two buildings was a good seven feet above the road.

That's what we should do, I thought, *instead of driving to the clinic at Snake Creek!* I held back the urge to jump out and join the Ashburns at the packinghouse. As I watched, the roof of the Islamorada train station blew into the air, tumbling and turning in the powerful wind.

A branch from a lemon or lime tree plunged onto the roof of the cab, its sharp thorns slicing across my face. I felt the warm trickles of blood and dove under the canvas again.

At times the truck slipped in the watery road, and I held my breath as we bounced and skidded our way north toward Snake Creek. Would we make it? I thought of the Bible story I heard at Sunday school, when Jesus calmed the Sea of Galilee just by saying, "Peace. Be still." I closed my eyes and prayed, "Please calm this storm. Make it end."

I hid under the tarp, shuddering with fear that we would be blown away or that something huge would fall on us. I crouched there until the truck stopped and Dad opened the cab door. "We made it!" he shouted. "Are you all right, Jake?"

"I'm okay," I said, throwing aside the canvas and climbing out onto the muddy road. "How is Star?"

"The same," Mom answered, opening her door. "Take her, Jake."

I gathered my little sister into my arms. She seemed so small and helpless. "Oh, God, please save my sister," I whispered.

Lantern lights gleamed through the upstairs windows of the two-story hotel that had been turned into the veterans' hospital, and I could see shadows of people.

Dad took Star from me and raced ahead of us. "We need a doctor right now!" he yelled. Inside the building the water was over our ankles, and I understood why the lights were only shining from the second-floor windows. Dad took the stairs two at a time, and Mom and I dashed after him. "My daughter needs a doctor immediately!"

A man who seemed to be in charge stepped toward us. "I'm Dr. Lassiter," he said. "We sent all our patients and staff away in the ambulances before the storm set in. I'm the only doctor left on the island, and we're busy with injuries and refugees."

"But we're refugees," Dad argued, "and my baby here is delirious with fever. It's been going on for days now. She needs medical help."

"I'll take a look at her," the doctor said, pointing to a cot, "but there's not much we can do. The power is off now, and we're not equipped to handle anything that could be serious."

"Please help us," Mom begged. "I think she has the sleeping sickness."

Dad placed Star gently onto the cot. Star murmured something but continued to sleep.

Dr. Lassiter put his hand to Star's forehead, looked under her eyelids, and then listened to her heart with the stethoscope. "She's comatose. It does look like encephalitis," he agreed.

"Do you have any medication to break the fever?" Mom asked.

"There's nothing I can do right now. Try to keep her cool," the doctor said. "We've got to get through this hurricane, and then we'll decide what steps to take for your child." He shook his head, and his eyes were sad. "I'm sorry."

Mom sat on the cot, put her hands over her face, and wept, while Dad patted her shoulder. Dr. Lassiter walked over to a man who had just arrived. At that moment the hospital trembled as a gust of wind blew out a window. The people who huddled together cried out.

"This building will go!"

"We've got to get out!"

"Where can we find a safe place?"

Dr. Lassiter clapped his hands for silence. "I've just heard the rescue train will be coming through any time now," he shouted. "It's scheduled to head south to Camp Three on Lower Matecumbe Key, pick up the veterans there, and then turn around and head north to Miami. Some folks are already out on the tracks to stop the train when it comes over the bridge. They figure they'll be safe in the train, even though it's heading south first. Perhaps that's where you should go before this building collapses."

Some families jumped up and ran for the stairway. "Keep order!" the doctor called after them. "Don't panic!"

Dad lifted Star over his shoulder. "Let's go," he said.

We went down the stairs, waded out into the wild night, and climbed back into the truck. This time it wouldn't start. "Never mind," Dad said. "The tracks are just up the road."

The storm was so strong that we had to fight and push our way against the wind as we struggled toward the railroad tracks. We also had to watch out for flying debris and falling trees. Several times the heavy gusts pushed Mom to her knees, and I took her hands and pulled with all my strength to get her up. Eventually we climbed up the railroad bed and onto the tracks. The Snake Creek train-station house was gone, and men were busy pulling debris from the rails while families with children clustered together anxiously waiting for the train.

"Oh, please, dear God," a woman cried. "Protect us from the storm."

"Get us to safety," added another voice.

We bowed low against the blasts of wind, and from where we stood above the road, the lightning revealed the outline of the hospital clinic. Suddenly, as if it were made of toy blocks, the building fell apart in pieces and rattled off through the air. We clung together in the downpour and the wind, while Windley Key was ripped apart in front of our eyes.

"Listen!" a man yelled. "I hear the train!"

Sure enough, a loud whistle and the chugging of a steam engine could be heard above the roar of the wind.

"Thank God!"

"Make the train stop!"

"Stand out on the tracks and wave your oilskins!" came the shouts. Between gusts that nearly knocked me over, I struggled onto the tracks, tore off my yellow slicker, and signaled. The train was coming, but we didn't see the light from the locomotive.

Then Dad shouted, "Stay back, Jake! Look out! The engine is in the back, and the engineer won't see you!"

Dad was right. The coach cars were in the front, and the locomotive was in the rear of the train. But it didn't matter. Someone must have seen us, because the train came to a stop, and the people along the tracks ran through the rising water for refuge in the large, heavy coaches.

"The engine is pushing the passenger cars to save time on the return to Miami," Dad explained as we climbed on board one of the coaches. "When it heads back north it will already be in the front of the train."

"But we have to head all the way back to Islamorada first, and then down to Lower Matecumbe for the vets down there at camp 3," I said. "By the time we come back through here, the bridges may be out."

"Don't worry, Jake. We'll be safe in the train," Mom said. "Just get inside and turn a seat out for Star."

There were no passengers on the train; obviously it had been sent empty to make room for the refugees. We settled ourselves toward the middle of the nearest car. Dad and I sat together, and Mom faced us, with Star snuggled close to her. Star's eyes seemed to be lost in dark circles, and she lay so quietly that it frightened me. Then she sighed, and I knew she was still with us.

Star, I thought, *I would give anything in the*

world to hear your sweet chatter. Tears welled up in my eyes. *Please, dear Lord, save my sister.*

The engine began to roar, the whistle blew eerily, and then very slowly the train started to chug its way down to Islamorada. Driving rain pelted the window, but in the flashes of lightning that filled the sky I could see the outlines of uprooted trees, and flat, empty land that looked like a desert.

"Why are we going so slowly?" Mom asked.

"I think the tracks are covered with water and debris, but I can't tell from here," I said, squinting out the window. "I'll go out onto the platform and take a look."

"Be careful, Jake," Mom said.

The coach trembled in the violent wind, and I had to force the door open between our car and the one behind us. I clutched the door and the handrails, praying I would not be blown over. Looking down at the tracks, I could see that the water had risen higher than the wheels of the train. The island was underwater.

The train's whistle blew over and over, and I could see the familiar faces of the townsfolk who huddled alongside the tracks, screaming for the engineer to halt. The locomotive pushed the cars beyond the crowd and came to a stop. We were back in Islamorada! The refugees from the storm sloshed up to their waists in water to get aboard. I wondered if Mara was somewhere in the crowd.

As the frightened locals crowded on board, I pushed my way back to where my family was seated. The sea was sweeping into the car around our feet.

"Hurry!" called the conductor as he helped women and children on board. "We've got to get on a side rail to the water tower. The boiler is almost empty, and the train won't make it to Miami without water. We still have to get down to Camp Three! This train has been sent by the government especially for the veterans, you know."

"You can't leave other citizens behind!" a man yelled.

"That's why we stopped for you," the conductor called out angrily. "Get a seat and—" The rest of his words were cut off by the earsplitting shrieks of wind.

I sat next to Dad, who was peering anxiously

out the window. "It's hard to see, but it looks like the water has risen."

"It has, Dad," I told him. "These people who were waiting on the railroad bed were already up to their knees in water."

As the conductor walked by, Mom grabbed his arm. "Can the train still move?"

"As long as the water doesn't reach the boiler and put out the fire and steam," he answered.

Mom and Dad looked down at the train floor and then at each other. The floors inside the coach were now ankle-deep in water.

"We're going to head for the side rail to fill the boiler!" the conductor announced. "Keep the doors shut."

The whistle blew again, and we could hear the sound of the throttle roaring, but nothing happened.

"The brakes won't release. The water has jammed them," Dad said. "I'll bet that's what's happened." He got up and ran out, back toward the locomotive engine.

Mom reached over and held on to my hand

and I could see hopelessness in her eyes. All the while, our little Star slept on as sweetly as if she were in her own bed.

When Dad returned and opened the door between the cars, a gush of water followed him into the coach. His pale face stood out in the gloom. "The brakes are locked."

Suddenly a man rushed in from the forward car and dove behind a bench. "The sea is on top of us!" he screamed.

Dad and I looked outside the window, where the lightning made the sky as bright as noonday, and I saw a rising, moving horizon that I would relive in my nightmares forever.

"Oh, my God!" Dad's voice shook, and he grabbed Star in his arms. "Hang on!"

People screamed and pointed with shaking fingers toward the windows that faced the east.

"Look!"

"Oh, my dear Lord!"

"Our Father who art in heaven . . ."

"We're all goners!"

"Let's get out," Dad exclaimed, "or we'll be

trapped in here." He grabbed Star with one arm and shoved Mom toward the door with the other.

Would we be safer outside? I had no time to make a decision. I followed my parents as they jumped off the train into the rising water. But it was too late for me. I was still inside the train as the gigantic wall of foaming, angry water roared toward us!

The monster from the sea charged upon us with the sound of a billion oceans combined with the screams of those of us trapped inside the train. The powerful wave hit, lifting our heavy passenger car off the tracks. A gigantic barrage of water poured through the broken doors and windows of the coach. It seemed as if the entire ocean were upon us as I felt myself underwater—somersaulting and turning, flung against the walls and smashed against the seats. Bodies floated and flailed around me. My lungs were bursting and I tried to breathe, but I only gulped in salt water. I was drowning..

Then the passenger car bumped and shook and settled on the ground. As if a plug had been pulled in a tub, the water inside began slithering out through the open places, pulling me along in the current, sucking me through some opening, and then hurling me into the air.

I don't know how long I was out cold, but in the early hours of the morning I awoke and found myself cradled in the broken bough of a tall gumbo-limbo tree. It seemed I was at least twenty feet off the ground. As the giant wave receded, it must have lifted me up into the limbs. The wind howled in gusts through the leafless branches, but the storm had passed. I was hurting everywhere, and I had stinging cuts all over me.

"Star! Star!" I screamed hoarsely over and over. "Mom! Dad!" There was no answer. I put both my arms around the trunk of the tree as if it were my only friend in the world, and I began to sob.

As dawn came, the horror of the storm surrounded me. Where was I? I knew I must be in Islamorada, but this place was some strange desert that was as desolate as the moon. I could barely discern what was left of the packinghouse. The timbers and shingles were scattered over the embankment where the train tracks had been. What had happened to the Ashburns, who had gone to the packinghouse for safety?

The Millionaires Club and the hotel were gone completely. Some houses remained, but they'd been moved or had been wrecked so badly they were indistinguishable. I strained to see where our house had been. All I could make out were scattered piles of rubble. Then I turned toward Miss Edith's house—the one that had been anchored so securely to the rock coral beneath it. Except for one wall, there was nothing left.

Seaweed and litter hung from the branches of other trees, where the giant wave had tossed them. I shuddered at the sight of a torn orange apron draped across the fronds of a palm tree. "Oh, no! No! Miss Edith!" I screamed in panic. My stomach knotted and I began to cry.

Then I thought of Mara. I scanned the other trees that were still standing, praying she was not there, praying she was alive.

Had my family survived? "Mom! Dad!" I called, not recognizing my own trembling voice. "Star!" I was stabbed with pains everywhere, and finally I slipped into darkness and let it take me to a far-away peaceful place.

Later when I awoke again, I realized that

beyond my pain I was alive, at least. Where was my family? They had made it out of the coach before the wave hit, but where were they?

I glanced toward Miss Edith's tattered apron, which swung silently on the nearby tree. I remembered that Mara had feared something was about to end. She had been right. "Mara!" I yelled to the empty sky.

I had to get down! I had to find out if Mom and Dad and Star had survived. I would never forget all the times I'd teased my little sister and called her a pest. Now I would give my own life to find her safe. "Star! Star!" I called into the air. "Please, God. Let her be all right."

I saw a few people staggering around as if in a trance.

"Help me!" I called. If they heard me, they were in such pain or so stunned, they never looked up. *I must get down and find my family*, I thought.

The ground looked so far away. I couldn't jump without breaking bones. There were large branches lower on the tree, and I began to descend. Once I got to the lowest branch, perhaps I would be able to shimmy down. "Dad! Mom!" I called. Over by the black shadow of the upturned passenger car I could hear faint cries. Were people still trapped inside?

"Jake!" My dad's voice! He was limping as he ran toward me. "Are you all right?"

"I'm okay. Where's Mom? Where's Star?"

"Mom's hurt, and Star is pinned down under a timber from the packinghouse. I can't get her out by myself."

"I'm coming down, Dad." I scrambled down through the branches. "Stay below me."

Dad ran to the base of the tree and looked up at me. "Come ahead, Jake. You can do it."

From where I was on the lowest bough, it was about fifteen feet to the ground. I could jump fifteen feet, couldn't I? But I decided to slide down the trunk instead. Dad stood below, watching. I noticed a cut on his forehead that had bled until his shirt was drenched. "Are you okay?"

"I'm all right. But Mom is hurt pretty bad— broken leg and God knows what else."

"And Star?"

"I can't get to her, so I don't know how badly she's hurt." I was close enough to see the deep worry in Dad's eyes. I wrapped my legs around the trunk and descended quickly. I had to help Mom and Star. As soon as my feet touched the ground, I was in my father's arms. "Thank God you're alive, Jake." His voice broke and we held on to each other for several moments.

"Let's go to Mom and Star," I said. "Where are they?"

"The wave dropped us near the packinghouse."

"The Ashburns went there. Did you see them?"

Dad nodded. "The family made it there before the heft of the storm hit. But the ocean roared all the way up there, too, and hit the building full force. Roy was washed away. They're searching for him now."

I had to see my mother and sister now. "Let's get to Mom and Star. Quick!"

We plodded over limbs and trees until we came near the remains of a water-soaked chair, where Mom was stretched out. Her face was swollen and bruised. She held her arms awkwardly, and one leg was folded to the side. "Oh, Mom!" I ran to her to hug her, but she moaned, "Don't touch me, Jake. I'm hurting so badly, and I think I've broken several bones." She seemed too dazed to cry, but she murmured, "Jake." I bent down to her, and she kissed me over and over. "Go help Star," she whispered.

"She's over there." Dad and I raced to the railroad bed, where a wall of the packinghouse lay tipped on its side. Broken boxes were spilled everywhere, and flies were already buzzing and gathering around the rotten fruit. When we came to a large timber that crossed our path, Dad pointed to a hole under the tracks where the water had washed the earth away. "Star's under there. It's the central beam of the packinghouse. If we could just move that timber, we could get to her."

"Did it land on her?" I was afraid to look.

"I don't think so. The beam isn't directly on her. But if we move it, I'm afraid it could fall on her—or the earth could cave in and she'd be smothered."

I bent over and could see just a glimpse of her blond hair and her little hand. "Star! It's me, Jake." My voice was tight and I could hardly speak. "We're coming to get you, Star."

When there was no answer, my heart broke in two. "I love you, Star. I'm going to get you out, my twinkle star." *Please, God,* I prayed silently, *let her be alive. Help me to get her out somehow.* "I'm strong, Dad," I said. "Together we should be able to move it."

"Thank God she fell into that cavity. Otherwise . . ."

"Come on, Dad. Let's give it a try." I tried to ignore my own pain and the blood oozing from the deep scratches on my legs.

We each took an end of the timber. "Hold on tightly," Dad said. "For God's sake, Jake, don't drop it. If it falls, it will crush Star. And stop immediately if any earth begins to fall on her." Dad counted. "One, two, *three!*" We strained to lift the heavy shaft of wood that trapped my sister, but we couldn't budge it. Dad looked defeated. "There's no way we can move that beam."

Then I thought of Jewel. "Jewel could do it!" I exclaimed. "I've seen her pull boats out of the water as if they were toys! If we can get Jewel, I know she'll help us."

"Go! I'll stay with Mom."

I turned and began to run toward Sharkey's place.

"We don't have much time, Jake," Dad called after me. "Hurry!"

Jewel is sturdy, and Sharkey would have protected her from the storm, I told myself. *They're both all right. I know they are. Even with his bad leg, Sharkey's a strong man. And Jewel is powerful. She can lift that beam. They'll help us. They've got to help us!*

I could hardly recognize where I was as I ran to Sharkey's. Familiar trees were gone; the pathways that I'd always used were filled with seaweed and broken branches. I had hoped the side of the island that faced Florida Bay was more protected, but the great wave that had come over the island from the ocean had washed straight through to the other side.

When I arrived at Sharkey's, I stopped in alarm. The boxcar was tipped over on its side; the sliding door, now on the top, was closed. I looked around the area, and there was no sign of Jewel.

"Sharkey!" I yelled, hoping to hear Rudy's happy barking, which always greeted me when I showed up. But there wasn't a sound.

I climbed onto what was now the top of the

boxcar and tugged at the doors. "Sharkey! Sharkey!"

Then I heard a thumping from inside. "Jake!" came a muffled voice.

"Are you okay? I'm trying to get you out, but the doors are jammed."

"I've been trying to clear the bent metal with this pry-bar." I heard a grating sound and pounding—along with some grumbling curses. "Now let's try together!" Sharkey yelled. "One, two . . ."

I yanked at the doors again and again until they began to slide apart. Sharkey and I pushed and tugged until they were wide open. I peered down into the topsy-turvy freight car. Sharkey stared up at me from the shadows below. I could make out water and debris on the bottom, where the sea had pushed its way in. Sharkey was standing on a table and holding the lever he'd used to push at the doors. Standing below him was Jewel.

I couldn't help but laugh with relief. "You brought Jewel into your house!"

"Of course. I wouldn't leave her out in that storm." Sharkey looked miserable. "But I have bad news, Jake. Poor Rudy . . ." His eyes filled up. "When we tipped over, the heavy chest of drawers by my bed fell on him."

"What are you saying?"

"He's gone, Jake." Sharkey shook his head and turned away.

My heart sank. "Oh, no. I'm sorry, Sharkey." Then, as sad as I was, I knew I had to push on. I had very little time to save Star. "Please help me save my sister. She's trapped under a heavy piece of timber. Only Jewel can lift it, Sharkey. Hurry! Bring Jewel and come."

Sharkey wiped his nose on his shirt. Then he nodded. "We'll need a plank of some sort to get out of here."

"I'll look for something." I dashed around searching for a piece of flat timber. The clutter of the storm was everywhere. The old shed was gone. The corral fencing had disappeared. The dock had been tossed up onto the land nearby. Two sections looked about the right size and width for Jewel to get out. I ran back to Sharkey, who was already pulling himself out of what was now the top of his shelter. "Help me bring the dock."

Sharkey slid out of the boxcar carrying Jewel's harnesses and a block and tackle. He looked around at the devastation in dismay, hoisted himself down to the ground, and then walked lamely over to me. I could tell from his limp that his leg must be hurting badly. Nevertheless Sharkey and I were able to carry the pieces of the dock over to the boxcar. We set one section up as a ramp from the ground to the doors of the boxcar. Then from the open doors we pushed one end of the second plank down into the opening, making another ramp for Jewel to get out.

I made my way down into the dim interior. There was Jewel standing over a small dark form—Rudy, who lay on his side, still and silent. I swallowed back my sadness, took hold of Jewel's bridle, and led her to the ramp. "Come on, Jewel. Up you go," I said gently. But Jewel would not move. "You've climbed up steep planks in your life, haven't you, girl?" I murmured. "Star needs you. Come on, come on."

Then I remembered. Jewel needed Rudy. Rudy

was her faithful buddy. They'd gone together through the fearful wild storm, and now all she wanted was for her friend to be with her.

I went back and gathered Rudy into my arms and held him in front of Jewel. Jewel sniffed at the dog and whinnied. "It's all right, girl. Come on." I couldn't hold on to the mule's lead and carry Rudy too. "Follow me, Jewel. Rudy's here, see?" Still holding Rudy, I climbed up the ramp. "Please, Jewel. Please help us," I begged.

When I reached the doors at the top of the boxcar, I looked back. Jewel was placing a hoof tentatively onto the incline. After testing it out, she began her ascent to the daylight above.

"We're coming," I said to Sharkey, who waited on the ground by the second ramp with Jewel's harness and the rope and tackle he would need to lift the beam off Star. "We need to get to Star right away," I said. "But Jewel won't go without Rudy, so I have to take him with us."

As we headed back to Star, I clutched Rudy's limp form in my arms. His once-beautiful tail was matted with water and seaweed.

Sharkey and Jewel followed close behind me.

Back at the site near the old packinghouse I laid Rudy down where Jewel could see him. Sharkey hitched Jewel into her harness. I knew we hadn't really tricked Jewel into believing Rudy was alive; Jewel was the smartest mule in the world, wasn't she? The sorrow in her eyes made me sure we weren't fooling her. But something made her willing to help. Did she sense our fear and anxiety? For whatever reason, Jewel stood silent and willing.

Mom had slipped into a deep sleep. "She's in a state of shock," Dad said after taking her pulse. "I'm glad she's sleeping and not feeling pain for a while. Surely the word is out that we need doctors and medical care. But where are they?" His voice rose. "They'd better get here soon before . . ." He shook his head and looked away.

Sharkey stood below a nearby tree that had leafless branches. "This looks strong," he said. "I've got to get this rope up and around a sturdy limb to use for leverage." He swung the rope over and over, and finally it hooked onto a tree branch. He tested it, pulling the rope until it was stretched tight. "As we lift the beam and that end of the rope shortens through the tackle, Jewel will pull, keeping the rope taut. When Jewel stops, the gears in the tackle will lock, keeping the timber from slipping back." He fastened the rope and tackle onto Jewel's harness, and the other end to the timber. "Now if you two can balance each end so the timber won't tip and slide out of the knotted rope, we're all set. Right, Jewel?" He patted Jewel's neck. "Jake, you stand near one end, and Doug, you stand by the other. If it tips at all, you'll need to level it. It'll take a lot of strength. Can you both handle it?"

"We'll do it, no matter what!" Dad vowed. "Right, Jake?"

"Right!" I moved to my end and got into position with a wide stance. "We're coming, Star!" I hollered. "We're coming."

"At the same time we need to be sure the hole doesn't cave in on Star." Dad warned. "So watch for any movement."

Sharkey went to Jewel and turned her so she was facing the other direction, away from the hole where Star was caught. "Here we go, Jewel. Haul!" Jewel tightened her muscles and began to tug her burden. "You can pull that hunk of wood, Jewel. Pretend it's just our old rowboat." Sharkey slapped Jewel lightly on her flank. "Haul, girl!" he commanded. "Haul!" Jewel strained, bending her head forward as she heaved the heavy beam. "Pull. Come on, Jewel, you can do it," Sharkey urged her on.

Gradually the timber moved and lifted. I held my breath, watching to be sure my end didn't tip or fall. At times the giant beam swayed. "Halt! Whoa!" Sharkey yelled, and he tightened the rope and we did our job of balancing. As if she understood, Jewel pulled the rope with cautious, sure-footed strides until the beam was up and turned away from the pile of debris where Star was trapped.

"Good girl, Jewel!" I yelled as we guided the beam safely to the ground far from my sister.

We flew to Star. "You're almost out, honey," Dad said to her.

She didn't answer. I could see her little hand, the fingers bent and still. Star was curled up amidst rubble, her eyes closed, her hair matted with blood and dirt. My throat tightened. Was she alive? *Lord, please let her live,* I prayed silently.

I stood back as Dad lifted her from the debris. He brushed a strand of hair from her face. Under the tangled hair we could see a welt and a deep cut. He kissed her. "Estelle," he whispered. "Our little Star."

I looked around for something for her to lie on and recognized a broken stool and other wrecked furniture that had been blown away from our house. Then I tripped over a chunk of soaking wet fabric. Mom's genuine American Oriental rug! It was heavy with seawater, but I was able to drag it back and lay it on a smooth section of wet ground. At least it was soft.

"Do you hurt, sweetheart?" Dad asked her.

Star didn't answer, but her eyelids fluttered open. She stared up, her eyes empty and without expression. "Star, it's me, Jake," I said, bending over her. But that vacant, empty look hit me like a blow to my stomach. "She doesn't know me!"

Dad's eyes were filled with anguish as he placed her gently on the rug. "Just rest, honey," he whispered.

I bent over my sister and sang softly to her. "Twinkle, twinkle, little Star. I love you just the way you are." I kissed Star's pale cheek and tasted salt from my own tears that had dropped onto her face. "I love you, Star. I love you more than the world. Please come back to us."

When Sharkey was ready to go, he placed Rudy's body on Jewel's back and led them away. "I need to find a place to bury Rudy," he said when he left. "If any of you want to stay in my over-turned house, you're welcome."

I noticed that Jewel trudged along sorrowfully through the rubble, her head bowed and her eyes sad. Sharkey led her slowly, looking old and anguished, with stooped shoulders and a gloomy, lined face. "Jewel and I will go around town—or what's left of it—to see if there's anything we can do to help out," he told us.

My mother suffered terribly the night after the storm. We slept outside—there was nowhere else to go, since we couldn't move Mom to Sharkey's. I stayed up most of the night, fending off mosquitoes.

Finally Dad used some rags and gas he found and made a smudge pot of smoldering embers. I could see smoke from other smudge pots rising against the evening sky. Later, kerosene lanterns burned here and there, and I could hear cries of people in mourning or in pain. They joined in with my mother's moans, and together it made a sad music that echoed on the barren island.

But Star was silent. She just lay on the old rug and stared at the sky.

Since the bridge at Snake Creek was destroyed, the Red Cross medical teams came by seaplane early on Wednesday. One of their nurses, Addie O'Brien, a brisk but kind lady, found us. She gave Mom pills for pain relief until they could get her to an ambulance and hospital. Mom was so badly hurt that she was one of the first on the list of injured who needed immediate medical attention. "She must have surgery as soon as possible," the nurse told us.

Addie examined Star. "She has no fever now," she told Dad, "but she doesn't respond to any stimulus. This child needs to get to the hospital."

She washed Star with water she brought, cut her hair, and then cleaned and bandaged her head.

Addie checked me out too, looking down my throat and into my eyes with a light. She put antiseptic on my legs where I cut them shimmying down the tree, and she bandaged my arm, which was bruised and swollen. "Let's stitch up your forehead," she ordered.

I touched my head and felt the sticky remains of blood and jagged flesh. "I didn't know I had a cut there," I told her. "Can't you just wash it off and put on a bandage?"

"No." She pulled out a needle and catgut and stitched me up. I was too tired to argue, and besides, it didn't hurt too badly.

She worked on Dad, too, stitching up the wound on his head and one on his shoulder. "Your wife and daughter need immediate attention," she told him, "and you must come as their next of kin. But your boy here will have to stay. We have no room for him on the plane."

"I can't leave Jake behind," Dad said. "He's got to come with us. He can't stay here in this god-forsaken place by himself."

"It's okay, Dad," I insisted. "I'll stay with Sharkey. I can be of help here."

"Is he well enough to be here on his own?" Dad asked Addie. "He's so young, and the island is so badly destroyed. There's no water . . ."

"Your son's injuries are superficial and should heal on their own," she answered. Then, turning to me, she said, "There's a whole tank car filled with drinking water at the railroad siding. It was the regular water delivery for the town. The train hauled it here just before the hurricane. It's a godsend. Everyone can use it. You'll need a clean container to store it, Jake."

"I'll be careful, Dad," I promised. "You've got to take the plane with Mom and Star. Don't worry about me. Sharkey and I will be okay."

Dad looked distressed, but he finally agreed. "I'll come back to get you as soon as I can—once the bridges are repaired."

Addie shook her head. "No guarantee when that will be."

"Then I'll come by boat," Dad replied.

Within an hour or so a group of men arrived with stretchers and carried Mom and Star to the shore, where a boat would take them to the plane. I walked beside them, holding Star's hand and feeling sick inside. Would this be the last time I'd see my little sister or my mother?

"Will they get well?" I asked the doctor who was at the makeshift dock where the boat waited.

"I hope so, son," he said, patting my shoulder. "Pray for them."

"I'll need to know how Mom and Star are doing." Suddenly tears sprang up in my eyes, and I threw myself in my father's arms.

"I'll find a way to let you know how they are." He pushed me away gently and put out his hand. I knew Dad was counting on me to be brave as we shook hands. "Be strong, Jake."

When I kissed Mom good-bye, she whispered, "I love you, Jake," and struggled to smile. Then I gave Star a kiss on her pale cheek and waited for a response, but she kept her eyes on the sky and didn't know I was there. "Please come back to me, Star," I whispered.

Mom and Star were lifted into the boat, and Dad got in close behind them. I stood alone and watched as the craft made its way through the storm wreckage out to the waiting seaplane. When Dad waved good-bye as he climbed into the plane, I swallowed hard to hold back the tears.

The small plane lifted off and headed north. *They'll be in the hospital soon,* I told myself. *They'll be okay. I'll keep busy and help other folks, as Dad said,* I repeated over and over. *I'll find Mara. She'll be alone and scared.*

I turned away and walked through the desolate place that had been our beautiful island home. I had to find Mara. But there was no sign of her anywhere.

A group of men came and, with Jewel's help, were able to right Sharkey's boxcar. Then we cleaned it up and threw out items that had been ruined by the tidal wave. We ate out of cans over an outdoor fire and slept on blankets the Salvation Army gave us. They gave us clothes and shoes, too, that people on the mainland had donated, so we burned our dirty, bloody clothes in the fire. I was glad at night for the pants and long-sleeved shirt that kept the mosquitoes off my legs and arms.

Sharkey had trouble finding enough soil to bury Rudy, whom he had wrapped in a blanket. "The soil was washed away in the storm," he said. Finally we discovered a sandy stretch under the sapodilla tree near Sharkey's place that was deep enough. Jewel stood by as Sharkey pushed a shovel into the sand.

When we were finished digging, Sharkey placed Rudy gently into his grave. "Farewell, my friend," Sharkey said in a shaky voice. "You were a good dog."

Neither of us spoke as we filled Rudy's resting place with dirt and sand. When we were through, I placed a palm frond on the site—a kind of memorial flower. "Good-bye, Rudy," I said. "We'll miss you."

Sharkey just stood there silently by the grave, his eyes closed and his old hat in his hand.

A little later we headed back to Sharkey's place, and I glanced back. Jewel was standing by Rudy's tree. "Come on, Jewel," I called.

But Jewel wouldn't move away from Rudy's grave.

By Thursday after the hurricane, there was talk that the government would cremate the dead that had not been claimed or taken to cemeteries on the mainland. Our Matecumbe Key was a sad, pitiful place, and every moment when I wasn't giving Sharkey a hand, I searched for Mara.

No one knew how many people had died, since so many had been swept out to sea. Some were found, cast like seaweed onto the shore, and others were gone forever. I walked by the train that had come too late to rescue the veterans. Scores of men, women, and children had drowned, trapped inside the railroad coaches. We had escaped in the nick of time. And now the Flagler railroad, the eighth wonder of the world, was destroyed.

Boy Scouts arrived by boat to help carry bodies

to a morgue that had been set up. I didn't know how they could do it. I hung around outside the morgue to see if a redheaded girl around fourteen had been brought in. "There's no one here by that description," I was told.

I scanned the waterfronts several times, looking for a sign of Addie, the Red Cross nurse, hoping she'd bring good news about Mom and Star. But I stayed as far away from the wharves as I could because that's where many of the dead were waiting to be sent to Miami for burial.

From the distance I could see the bodies being lifted onto boats. I had heard that my friend Roy was one of them. Each time I thought about him and how we grew up fishing and swimming together, I got a sick feeling in my stomach.

On Friday morning after the storm I saw the Red Cross boat pull up to a dock, and Addie climbed out and came up onto the shore.

"How is my mother?" I yelled as I ran up to her. "Did you see my sister?"

"Yes, Jake," she answered. "Your mom is recovering nicely from the surgeries, but she'll be in a brace for a long time. She sends her love, and

she wants you in Miami with the family. Your
father will be coming to get you in a few days."

"What about my sister?" I asked.

Addie looked serious. "She's recovering, Jake,
but she's still ... disoriented."

"Disoriented? What does that mean?" I
demanded.

"She doesn't respond to anyone or anything—
not even your parents. It could be a combination
of all that happened—her severe illness plus
shock from the hurricane."

I felt like my heart dropped down to my toes
when she told me that. "Will she get better?"

"Only time will tell." Addie must have seen the
fear on my face, because she went on to say, "Star
is alive, and where there's life there's hope. Be
thankful you all survived, Jake."

"I am thankful, but I can't help being scared for
my sister," I replied. "Do you visit the hospital in
Miami often?"

"Almost every day," she answered.

"I'm looking for a friend—a girl named Mara
Lynn Kraynanski. She's about fourteen and has
beautiful long red hair."

"I don't know of anyone who looks like that." She handed me a pad of paper and a pencil. "Write her name down." After I printed Mara's whole name, Addie put the paper in her bag. "I'll see what I can find out," she promised.

Later, when Sharkey and I made rounds about the old neighborhood to aid survivors, Jewel went along obligingly. But she wasn't the same old Jewel. As soon as we came back to Sharkey's, she headed for the sapodilla tree next to Rudy's grave, then stood there with her head hung low.

That afternoon Billy came over to Sharkey's place looking for me. It was the first time I'd seen him since the storm. He had a cast on his arm and looked so thin I hardly recognized him. I wasn't sure just what to say to him about his brother dying, so I just mumbled, "Hey, Billy. How are you doing?"

"Not good," he answered. "The doctor said I'm lucky to be alive." He looked away, and his eyes filled with tears. "But I don't feel lucky."

"I'm real sorry about your brother," I said softly. "We had good times together. I'll never forget Roy."

"Neither will I." Billy walked over to the tree where Jewel was standing. "Jewel made it, I see."

"Yeah, Jewel made it, but Rudy died. He's buried there." I pointed to the grave.

"He was a good dog."

"How about your dog, Ginger?"

"Ginger is okay," Billy said. "It's kind of strange. Roy died and Ginger lived." Billy stroked Jewel's head and neck. "I hear your mom and sister are in the hospital."

"Mom's in a brace, but she'll get better in time. Star doesn't respond to anybody. I'm real scared for her, Billy."

"I hope she'll be all right. Bessie's got bruises and cuts, and she's had bad nightmares, but she'll be okay. She asked about Star."

Sharkey came out and hobbled over to us. He put his arm around Billy's shoulders. "I'm sorry about your brother. How are you?"

"As good as I can be."

Sharkey petted Jewel's brown nose, and she leaned her head against his chest. "Jewel knows Rudy's gone and she's mourning for him. She never moves away from his grave."

I kicked at a coral rock. "I wish she'd go wandering or do something devilish like she used to."

The three of us chuckled a little, remembering Jewel's antics. Then I asked Billy, "Do you know what's happened to Mara?"

"I don't know," Billy answered. "Her aunt died."

"Yeah, I figured as much," I said, recalling Miss Edith's orange apron swaying in the tree.

"I came over to say good-bye to you and Sharkey," Billy said. "We're going to Miami today. We're taking Roy to the cemetery there, where there's a family plot."

We were all silent for a moment. Then I asked, "You'll be back, won't you?"

"I don't know. It doesn't feel the same here without Roy. My dad says our family will never be the same."

Sharkey nodded. "The Keys will never be the same, either."

Billy shook hands with Sharkey and me and then headed through the brush. "Bye, Sharkey. Bye, Jake," he said with a wave.

"Bye, Billy," we both called.

We watched as Billy made his way through the brush and debris. He looked older and different, and I knew that the storm had changed something else, too. We weren't kids anymore.

Saturday after the hurricane the Red Cross nurse waved to me, and I dashed over to meet her. "Your mother is coming along well, Jake. And Star is up and around a bit now."

"Does she recognize anyone? Does she play or speak?"

"She seems to recognize your mom and dad. She's progressing, and in time she may speak again."

In time she may *speak again?* I couldn't bear to think of my little sister not speaking or begging me to read to her. "What about Mara?" I asked. "Did you find her?"

"I checked several places. She's not in Miami, Jake. I'm sorry."

After the nurse left, I told Sharkey, "Mara is not in Miami."

Sharkey put his hands on my shoulders, looked me in the eyes, and said, "Jake, Mara's gone. It's time for you to give up searching for your friend and move on. She'd be the first one to tell you that."

"But her life was . . . unfinished," I argued.

"So were the lives of the others who died," Sharkey said. "Unfinished."

The mass cremation and a ceremony were to take place near Snake Creek around noon today. It was a few miles up the road to Snake Creek, and the only transportation I had was Jewel hitched up to Sharkey's wagon. We were going to go, but at the last minute Sharkey's leg was bothering him, and he decided not to. I felt I should stay nearby in case he needed me.

Instead I went down to the shore where the church had been. From there I could see Snake Creek to the north. There were many boats heading that way.

The water was calm, and sounds traveled over the surface. I waited and watched silently. Soon the sound of a bugle playing taps drifted toward me on the breeze. I could see a flash of fire, and I watched as a black spiral of smoke rose into the sky and hung there until it became part of the clouds. Rifle shots pierced the air, and I knew the ceremony was over.

Mara was not in that cloud. But Mara should have someone remembering her. Why, even Rudy had had a little ceremony at his grave. All those people up there in that black cloud—they had had their memorial, and the word had gotten around that a beautiful monument would be erected in Islamorada in their honor.

But what about Mara? She had come here with her big smile and her beautiful words and her kind heart. She had said that nothing was ever permanent, and she knew that being here was too good to be true. She whistled that lullaby tune all the time as if trying to hold on to her mother— wherever she was. Now Miss Edith was gone, and there was no family left to acknowledge that Mara had ever been on this earth. She wasn't among those that were in the cloud. Mara had simply been blown away.

I needed to do something special for her—

something that would say she'd been here and she was important to me.

In my pocket I had a pencil and pad of paper that had been in a Red Cross package, so I sat on the stump of a tree and began to write a poem for her. I remembered how we had joked about my use of the word "eloquent." Mara would be happy to know that at least I was trying.

I wrote my poem as I sat by the water and the black cloud kept rising and melting into the sky. "Unfinished" would be the title.

I didn't realize how long I stayed there, trying different words and then crossing them out. The sun moved from the ocean side over the island to the bay, and a wind blew up, capping the water with white foam.

When I finished, I went to the water's edge. "Mara, I'm glad Islamorada became your island home, even though it was only for a short time." I spoke softly in a croaky voice, and my eyes were wet. "My family became your family, Mara, and they'd be here with me if they could. So this is a private ceremony, just between us.

"I learned a lot from you—about being kind,

and about lullaby memories. I'd never noticed how beautiful the sea was until you pointed it out to me. I know the sea will be beautiful again.

"So I wrote a poem for you. Believe me, it was really hard to write . . . and it's not great, because I'm not a poet like you. But it's for you, Mara, and it's about you. And the words came right out of my heart." I cleared my throat and spoke the words of my poem.

> *There was no ending to Mara's song,*
> *And the melody seemed to be all wrong.*
> *Her story finished without a plot,*
> *And all the dreams that she had sought*
> *Floated away like blue balloons*
> *On half-remembered, whistled tunes.*

"I will remember you forever," I told Mara.

I ripped the paper into tiny pieces and flung them into the wind, where they skipped above the surface of the water, then scattered and blew away.

I ended up staying with Sharkey for more than a month. I kept in touch with my family through Addie, who brought messages to and from Dad.

Sharkey worked and kept busy even with that bad leg of his. There was something strong about Sharkey that kept me going too.

But the storm had taken its toll on him. Although he tried to be positive, I knew he was tired and resigned. He didn't scowl or snarl as he used to, and there were times when I would have been happy to have grumpy old Sharkey back.

Every so often I'd take a stroll with him when I was sure he didn't want to be alone. He couldn't walk far with his bad leg, but we'd wander down by the shore near his place and watch for signs that marine life was still okay. He perked up when a manatee swam by.

"I'm sure glad to see that old fellow," he said. "Thought for sure he was gone too."

One day I asked about the turtle nest. "I wonder if the babies ever made it. Star was so eager to see them when they hatched, but I suppose they got washed away like everything else," I said sullenly.

"Jake, turtles have been nesting since time began—long before you and me. And there'll be turtles and nests and hatchlings long after we're gone."

Jewel stayed around the sapodilla tree where Sharkey had buried Ruby. Jewel never roamed or tried to get away, and her sad eyes looked as if she were weeping. Sharkey often cleaned her eyes with some herbal stuff. I brushed her coat and mane daily. She liked that. She'd lift her chin for me to brush her neck. "You're such a good girl," I told her. She nickered softly, but I hadn't heard her funny bray in a long time.

The bridges north of us had finally been repaired, and one morning while Sharkey and I were eating breakfast—dry cereal that the Red Cross had handed out along with other supplies for survivors—we heard a familiar voice.

"Hey!" Dad appeared suddenly from behind Sharkey's hut.

"Dad!" I jumped up and ran to meet him. "I can't believe you're really here!"

"I thought it was time to get you back to Miami with us." Dad gave me a hug. "We've missed you, Jake."

"I've missed you too, Dad. How did you get here?"

"Red Cross got me a used car, and as soon as the bridges were fixed, I had to come down right away." Dad had a mischievous smile. "I have a surprise for you, Jake!" He beckoned to someone who must have been waiting in back of the house.

To my astonishment Mom shuffled toward me, walking unsteadily with crutches, smiling and crying at the same time. I went to her and she dropped a crutch to put her arm around my shoulders. As I held her, I could feel the stiff cast from her neck to her waist. "I feel like Jewel must when she wears a harness," she said.

"Mom," was all I could say, because I didn't

want to cry like a little kid. I hugged and kissed her gently. She was so thin and pale, it seemed she could break in two.

"Thanks for taking care of my boy," Mom said to Sharkey.

"Oh, he's taken care of *me*!" Sharkey said. "Don't know how I would have made it without him."

"Look who else is here," Dad said.

I turned and saw Star standing quietly by, sucking her thumb. "Star!" I bent down and drew her close to me. "My little twinkle star," I whispered as she snuggled into my arms. "She remembers me," I mouthed to my mother and father.

"It seems like she does," Dad whispered. "It's hard to tell."

She was as cute as ever in her blue overalls and white sneakers. Her blond hair was now cropped short, and tiny curls framed her face. With her rosy cheeks and sturdy body, she could have been a poster for a perfectly healthy child. But when I looked into her eyes and recognized that empty stare, an awful, sick feeling washed over me again.

We all sat down at the picnic table Sharkey

had built from scraps. "I have something for you, Star," Sharkey said, and he reached into the work-box he kept nearby. He pulled out one of the objects he'd whittled over the past several weeks.

"Remember the baby turtles, Star?" he asked as he handed it to her. "Here's one for you to keep."

Star took the beautifully carved little sculpture and turned it over and over in her hand. But she said nothing.

"Jake! I'm back!"

We looked around as Billy Ashburn, carrying a heavy basket, made his way through the broken bushes.

"Hi, Billy!" I exclaimed. "Come see my folks."

"How are you and your family, Billy?" Mom asked.

"They're doing as well as they can," Billy answered. "Bessie asks for Star all the time."

"We haven't been home since the storm," Dad said.

"We decided to come back, too," Billy said. "Couldn't wait once the bridges were repaired." He joined us and placed the basket on the ground by the picnic table. I could hear high-pitched yelps coming from inside. "Whatcha got in there?" I asked curiously.

"Something for Sharkey and Jewel," Billy said with a grin.

Whatever was in the basket was eager to get out, because it was squeaking and scratching, and the lid was popping up and down.

Billy opened the cover, and a dark red puppy peeked out. He lifted the wiggly little dog and handed it to Sharkey. "She's from our dog, Ginger. Rudy was her papa. We wanted you to have this puppy, Sharkey."

"She looks just like Rudy!" Sharkey said as he cradled the pup in his arms. The puppy wiggled constantly—then lifted her head and licked Sharkey's face all over. For the first time since the storm Sharkey laughed out loud—a real belly laugh. "Hey, Jewel, look what we have here!" He carried the pup to Jewel, who was standing beneath the sapodilla tree, and held it up to her. Jewel sniffed at the squealing puppy, then let out her loud horse-donkey honk.

Sharkey set the puppy down, and we watched as it raced around the place, sniffing everything in sight.

"What will you name her?" Mom asked.

"I think Ruby would be a good name for a girl," Sharkey said.

"She'll be another gem—like Jewel," Mom agreed.

Star seemed to be listening, her eyes on the dog.

The puppy scurried around Sharkey's washed-out yard, chasing after butterflies and bumping into things. Jewel brayed loudly and trotted after the little dog.

"Look at those two," Sharkey said. "I've got my hands full again."

"And you'll love every minute," Dad said with a wink at me.

"They'll be nothing but trouble." Sharkey's old grumpy voice was back.

"But Sharkey," I said, adding my two cents' worth, "good things come in pairs, you know!"

We were all laughing when our attention was drawn to Star, who stood nearby, watching the two animals.

The pup had discovered Jewel's trough, and she nearly fell in as she lapped up the water. Star trotted over to the puppy, bent down, and patted her head. Little Ruby leaped up, knocked Star onto the ground, and then jumped on her. Star struggled to stand but was knocked over again by the playful, wiggling pup, who licked her face over and over.

To our surprise and joy my little sister began to giggle.

"Ruby!" she said in the sweetest, clearest, most beautiful voice. "Ruby!"

EPILOGUE

For the next year I lived with my family in a small apartment in Miami and went to school there. But I missed my island home. And I missed Sharkey and Jewel, and Ruby, and my friend Billy, too.

Then we heard the good news that the Red Cross and others were building houses for twenty-eight families who survived the storm—and we were one of those families! I could hardly wait to move back!

When the big day came, Dad and I packed up our few belongings, while Mom gave directions. Star helped too, packing her own boxes, chattering all the time like her old self.

Our new one-story house was built of white concrete and stood alongside a row of other houses on a newly constructed side street. "This house will never blow away," Dad said as he looked everything over.

We discovered the cisterns stored water under the house. "No more rain barrels to clean," I said.

"And there are no stairs for me to climb." Mom was still in a brace and used a cane. She was over-joyed with her new kitchen with its shiny stove and refrigerator. "Think of all the family meals we'll have here together. How blessed we are just to be alive—and now we've been given this lovely home!"

"I suppose you'll want a new genuine Ameri-can Oriental rug," Dad said.

"No, I will not! There are more important things in life than a rug!"

Star raced through the house, checking every room, and then she went outside. "Come with me, Jake," she said. "Let's go find Sharkey and Jewel. And Ruby."

I took her hand, and we walked by the spot where our house and store had been.

"Our house is gone," Star said. "Blown away."

"But Dad's going to build a new store," I told her.

When we arrived where Sharkey's place had been, we stopped dead in our tracks. The freight car was gone, and in its place was a smaller version of our new house. Sharkey was outside planting fruit trees, while Jewel and Ruby meandered around.

Ruby, who had grown as big as Rudy, barked and ran to us, jumping and leaping around like crazy. Sharkey's face lit up when he saw us. "Welcome back, Jake! Let's go down to the water. I have something to show Star." He took Star's hand. Jewel and Ruby followed as the three of us walked to Sharkey's beach.

"It's not the same Islamorada," I said. "New houses, new bushes, new trees..."

"The railroad's gone forever," Sharkey said. "But folks will drive their cars down here on the highway once it's completed. The island will be part of the other world now."

As we stepped out onto the sandy beach, Sharkey pointed to a burrow of dirt and tiny scratch marks that led to the water. "The baby turtles have hatched, Star. See their little tracks heading right to the water?"

Star bent over to examine the marks on the sand where the hatchlings had made their way to the sea.

"So they're safe now?" she asked. "They're back in their own home?"

"That's right," I told her. "They're safe at home. And so are we."

That first night in our new house, Star called to me from her bedroom. "Jake! Look what Mommy bought for me." She held up a new copy of *Wind and Stars and Bright Blue Skies.*

I sat on her bed. "Would you like me to read it to you?" I asked.

"I want Mara to read it to me."

"But we told you that Mara's gone, Star," I said.

"I know. But where did she go?"

"Far, far away."

She handed the book to me. "How far is far, far away, Jake?"

"Beyond the wind and stars and bright blue skies," I told her.

AFTERWORD

My story *Blown Away!* is a work of fiction. The characters—both human and animals—were born from my imagination. But the hurricane and other elements in the story are based upon actual events that took place in Islamorada on Matecumbe Key, Florida, in 1935.

Islamorada, I've been told, means "purple isle." However, I also understand from Spanish and Portuguese friends that it can mean "island home" or "island abode." I've used the translation "island home" in my book.

You may wonder why the great Labor Day Hurricane of 1935 is now considered to be the "Storm of the Century." After all, throughout history Florida has been known for its powerful hurricanes. What made this one unique?

According to most records, the Labor Day

Hurricane of 1935 made landfall with the lowest barometric pressure that had ever been recorded. Officially the barometric pressure was 26.3 inches, but according to one survivor, his barometer dropped to 26.0 at the heft of the storm. At that point, in fear and surrender, he threw his barometer away. The sustained winds in this storm were recorded at 160 miles per hour, with gusts to more than 200 miles per hour. For fifty years it held the record as the strongest Atlantic hurricane. Readers who are interested in weather may enjoy using a simple barometer, and watching how barometric pressure changes from High (favorable weather) to Low (changeable) to Very Low (stormy).

The storm surge was great. A wall of water eighteen to twenty feet high, with waves up to thirty feet high, completely flooded Matecumbe Key. Some survivors felt that the high mound of earth that had been built for the train tracks acted as a dam, causing the seawater to build up even higher before engulfing the town of Islamorada.

The surge was so powerful that it overturned all the cars of the rescue train that was sent to save the veterans trapped on the island, except the locomotive itself. When the surge hit, one survivor was blown out of his cottage and into the flood. He awoke to find himself caught up in a tree twenty feet above the ground—like Jake in my story.

According to records, 423 people were killed by the hurricane, but many people were never found, so the actual number may be higher. Of the 718 veterans employed by the government, 350 had gone to Miami for a Labor Day baseball game; that trip may have spared them their lives.

In the 1930s meteorologists did not have the sophisticated scientific equipment available today to follow the courses of hurricanes. That may be the main reason the track of the hurricane was not properly forecast, which put many people in danger.

During the era when my story takes place, there was an epidemic of the mosquito-borne disease encephalitis, which was also known as sleeping sickness. This is the illness that made Star so sick. Often victims never fully recovered. Today insecticide sprays are used in many communities to control mosquitoes and the diseases they carry.

Were there panthers in the Florida Keys at the time of the 1935 Labor Day Hurricane? In my interviews with long-time residents of the Keys, I was told many stories about panthers that came to visit their islands in the past. In fact, a panther was recently sighted in the Keys.

Why did I choose a mule for my story? Mules had a great impact on the history of our country, and they have touched our lives in more ways than many of us know. Pack mules carried heavy loads as pioneers made their way westward, and mules towed boats along the canals. Maybe you've heard the old folk song:

> I've got a mule and her name is Sal,
> Fifteen miles on the Erie Canal.
> She's a good old worker and a grand old pal,
> Fifteen miles on the Erie Canal.

Mules also helped build the highways and railroads, such as the Flagler railway in my story, long before automobiles and trucks took over. They also worked—and continue to work—in the coal mines.

What makes mules different? They are hybrids—part horse, part donkey. Fortunately, they are made up of the best parts of both animals, which means they have extraordinary strength and patience. They are less excitable than horses, but they're sure-footed and have a great talent for jumping. Like Jewel in my story, mules can jump a high fence from a standing position; a horse needs a running start.

Mules are also extremely intelligent. You've probably heard the expression "stubborn as a mule." Mules are not actually stubborn, but they are smart enough to know when a situation is dangerous—and that's when they will refuse to budge.

Because mules are hybrids, they cannot reproduce colts of their own. This is rather sad, but it's part of the law of nature regarding hybrids. It's true, however, that a mule usually has a pal—like a horse or dog—that it loves and follows. That's how Rudy came to have a part in my plot.

Today mules are still used as working animals, but they are also used in sports such as hunting, racing, jumping, and trail riding. I hope that after reading my book, readers will have a new respect for this hard-working and intelligent animal.

The poems in this story were written by the author, including those in Star's fictional book *Wind and Stars and Bright Blue Skies,* which you won't find in a bookstore or a library—at least, not yet!

WITH GRATITUDE...

. . . to Kristina and Jules Olitski for the use of their Islamorada cottage, where I did most of my research while enjoying the beauty of that delightful island. Many thanks, Kris, my treasured friend, for your countless kindnesses, motivating support, and enthusiasm over the years.

. . . to Historian Jim Clupper, from the Helen Wadley Branch of the Monroe County Public Library in Islamorada, for sharing his wide range of knowledge of the Labor Day Hurricane, for use of the historical archives, and for patiently answering my many questions about the history and the early inhabitants of the Keys.

. . . for the pleasant and informative visit I had with Mrs. Alma Pinder Dalton and her sister, Dolores "Dorrie" Pinder Brothers, who as young children lived through the Labor Day Hurricane when many members of their friends and family perished or were seriously hurt. Sadly, Dorrie Pinder Brothers passed away just before this book was finished.

. . . and a ton of thankfulness to the staff at Moultonborough, New Hampshire, Library, who once again helped me with research, and use of their computers and fax. My New Hampshire friends and neighbors will enjoy visits to the new library wing, lecture hall, and especially the children's section with its beautiful murals of Lake Winnipesaukee.

. . . for the friendly assistance I have received from the reference staff at Venice (Florida) Public Library.

. . . to Mike and Deanna Sopko for graciously loaning me their prized collection of books on old Florida.

. . . to Carol, Elizabeth, June, and Gail—my loyal, talented, and supportive writing group—for cheering me on over the years.

. . . and many thanks to my understanding and gifted editor, Sarah Sevier, who edits my work with talent, care, and kindness.

. . . to Larry and Claire Krane, who offered an abundance of information about the coal mines and culm banks in Pennsylvania, the mules in the mines, and Polish cooking—and who assure me that free food has no calories!

Literature Circle Questions

Use these questions and the activities that follow to get more out of the experience of reading *Blown Away!* by Joan Hiatt Harlow.

1. Why does Jake feel guilty after he tries to protect the turtle nest on Sharkey's property?

2. What are the two definitions of the word "conch," according to Jake?

3. What is the special thing that Jake does for Mara after he accepts that she is gone forever?

4. What do the island kids think of Sharkey at the beginning of the book? Why?

5. What does Jake think is different or special about Mara? Choose an interaction between Mara and Jake and explain how it affects him.

6. Why does Sharkey finally decide to buy Jewel? What do you think this shows about Sharkey?

7. How does Jake feel about his sister early in the story? When does his relationship with Star start to change and why? How can you see that his relationship has changed?

8. Do you think Jake matures a lot over the course of the story? List the ways in which Jake changes.

9. What are the trials faced by Jake and his family during and after the hurricane? How do they face each difficulty?

10. Why is that "Genuine American Oriental Rug" so important to Jake's mom? How does she feel about it after the storm and why?

11. After the hurricane, some families return to the island and some do not. What are the reasons for each choice? Do you think Jake's family makes the right decision by coming back?

12. Imagine the story is told from Mara's perspective. How would it be different? What details would she include that Jake does not, and what would she leave out?

13. How do you think the residents of Islamorada could have been better prepared for the hurricane? Keep in mind that it is 1935 and they did not have the same weather prediction technology or resources that we have today.

14. The author chooses to include a funeral for Rudy the dog, but does not offer a neat conclusion to Mara's disappearance. Jake never finds out for sure what happened to his friend, and he can only assume that she was washed away during the hurricane. Why do you think the author leaves Mara's story open-ended?

15. Identify all the important people in Jake's life and list a lesson that he learns from each of them. Who do you think has the most influence on him during the course of the story?

Note: These questions are keyed to Bloom's Taxonomy as follows: Knowledge: 1–3; Comprehension: 4–5; Application: 6–7; Analysis: 8–11; Synthesis: 12–13; Evaluation: 14–15.

Activities

1. Imagine you are Mara, and it is the end of your first day in Islamorada. Write a journal entry describing your thoughts and feelings. Include impressions of life on the island, what you have seen and learned, and how you feel about the future. You can also include details about what has happened to you over the past month, and your feelings about your father's death and leaving your home in Pennsylvania.

2. It is ten years after the book ends, and Jake has taken over his parents' general store and lunch counter. Create a menu for the restaurant. Be sure to include illustrations and creative names for the dishes, and keep in mind that it is 1945 in the Florida Keys. You should do some research into what people were eating at the time and how much things cost, in order to make your menu historically accurate.

3. Draw a map of Jake's island. Include the town, the various characters' houses, Sharkey's place, Jewel's pen, the railroad tracks, the Florida Bay, and the Atlantic Ocean, as well as the places Jake goes fishing. Illustrate it with flora and fauna from the island, such as sea grapes, bonefish, gumbo-limbo trees, turtles, and a panther.

Other Novels by This Author

Joshua's Song
Midnight Rider
Shadows on the Sea
Star in the Storm
Thunder from the Sea

Date Due